BOOK THREE

SAINTED

USA TODAY BESTSELLING AUTHOR

HEATHER SLADE

sainted

/sane(t)ed/

verb

beyond reproach, or the process of
becoming that way

MORE FROM AUTHOR HEATHER SLADE

BUTLER RANCH
Kade's Worth
Brodie's Promise
Maddox's Truce
Naughton's Secret
Mercer's Vow
Kade's Return
Butler Ranch Christmas

WICKED WINEMAKERS
FIRST LABEL
Brix's Bid
Ridge's Release
Press' Passion
Zin's Sins
Tryst's Temptation

WICKED WINEMAKERS
SECOND LABEL
Beau's Beloved
Coming Soon:
Cru's Crush
Bones' Bliss
Snapper's Seduction
Kick's Kiss

ROARING FORK RANCH
Coming Soon:
Roaring Fork Wrangler
Roaring Fork Roughstock
Roaring Fork Rockstar
Roaring Fork Rooker
Roaring Fork Bridger

THE ROYAL AGENTS
OF MI6
Make Me Shiver
Drive Me Wilder
Feel My Pinch
Chase My Shadow
Find My Angel

K19 SECURITY
SOLUTIONS TEAM ONE
Razor's Edge
Gunner's Redemption
Mistletoe's Magic
Mantis' Desire
Dutch's Salvation

K19 SECURITY
SOLUTIONS TEAM TWO
Striker's Choice
Monk's Fire
Halo's Oath
Tackle's Honor
Onyx's Awakening

K19 SHADOW OPERATIONS
TEAM ONE
Code Name: Ranger
Code Name: Diesel
Code Name: Wasp
Code Name: Cowboy
Code Name: Mayhem

K19 ALLIED INTELLIGENCE
TEAM ONE
Code Name: Ares
Code Name: Cayman
Code Name: Poseidon
Code Name: Zeppelin
Code Name: Magnet

K19 ALLIED INTELLIGENCE
TEAM TWO
Coming Soon:
Code Name: Puck
Code Name: Michelangelo
Code Name: Typhon
Code Name: Hornet
Code Name: Reaper

PROTECTORS
UNDERCOVER
Undercover Agent
Undercover Emissary
Coming Soon:
Undercover Savior
Undercover Infidel
Undercover Assassin

THE INVINCIBLES
TEAM ONE
Decked
Edged
Grinded
Riled
Smoked

THE INVINCIBLES
TEAM TWO
Bucked
Irished
Sainted
Hammered
Ripped

THE UNSTOPPABLES
TEAM ONE
Furied
Merried

COWBOYS OF
CRESTED BUTTE
A Cowboy Falls
A Cowboy's Dance
A Cowboy's Kiss
A Cowboy Stays
A Cowboy Wins

Table of Contents

1

Harper

I flexed my hands, stiff from clenching my fists so hard there were nail marks in my palms.

I hated flying.

Not that I had much experience with it. Today was only the second time I'd been on a plane. The first, I wasn't alone like I was today. Then I'd been with my fiancé. The man who was supposed to become my husband. Keyword: *was.* As of this morning.

Since he wasn't, I was on a plane alone, sitting in first class with an empty seat beside me. Like that song by the country singer—I should get drunk. What was the line? Drink cheap champagne from a real glass? Except the glasses weren't real.

I swirled the ice melting in the plastic cup, wishing I'd asked for something stronger than soda. I'd tell the stewardess—flight attendant, as my ex-fiancé had corrected me on my first flight—I'd changed my mind, but she was otherwise engaged, talking to a ridiculously handsome man who'd just boarded the plane.

I couldn't blame her. He was hot. Beautiful, really. His sandy-blond hair looked just this side of shaggy, and his skin was tanned from the sun. When he spoke, though, God, that English accent!

It made sense he would be British, since I was on a nonstop flight to London.

London—where I was supposed to honeymoon with Douchey Dave, as my maid of honor, Mouse, had called him when she had to tell me he wasn't coming. He wasn't just late, hadn't been in a horrible accident, or gotten lost on the way to the church. He'd changed his mind. He didn't want to get married. Not today. Or any other day.

She'd convinced me I should go to London without him. "He paid for first-class seats; don't you dare let them go to waste," she insisted. She hadn't needed to say it twice. Although I would never admit it to her or anyone else, the real reason I showed up at the airport was that I thought Dave might too.

I closed my eyes and rested my head against the seat, shaking it at my own stupidity.

"Hello."

I opened my eyes and looked into the sapphire-blue ones of the gorgeous man with the English accent, who was putting something in the bin above my row of seats while the enraptured flight attendant held his drink.

The last thing I expected was for him to sit down in Douchey Dave's seat, but since the doors were now closed and locked, I had to accept the fact that my non-husband wasn't coming.

"Hello," I responded when he set his drink on the flat surface between our two seats, sat down, and fastened his seat belt. I pulled the emergency card from the seat pocket and listened as the woman—who couldn't tear her eyes from the man seated beside me—explained what passengers should do in the event of an emergency.

"You're the only person I've ever seen follow along, let alone pay attention," said my row mate.

"It's only my second time on a plane." I glanced with envy at the drink the Englishman nursed.

"And you're traveling all the way to London?"

"That's right."

"Brave girl."

"Not really," I mumbled. When it didn't appear he'd heard me and I saw him looking at something on his phone, I turned away and stared out the window.

"Bugger me," he muttered. Maybe his day was as bad as mine. Doubtful since I was going on my honeymoon without a husband.

I turned and held up my plastic cup when I heard the woman ask if she could bring another drink. Before I could respond, she was gone.

"Bad form," the man beside me said under his breath. "Did you want something?"

"Yes."

"What?"

"What what?"

He smiled. "Would you like?"

I bit my bottom lip. The main reason I hadn't ordered anything earlier was because I had no idea what to ask for. "Whatever you're having," I said when I saw the woman returning.

"Another, if you would, please." He pointed to his glass. "And a crack of champagne."

"Certainly," she said with a smile. For him. Not me. She hadn't looked at me since shortly after I boarded and she brought me a soda. I wasn't sure she'd glanced at me then, even when I thanked her.

She set both bottles and a fresh cup of ice in front of him, and he poured a little from each before handing it to me. "This is called a scotch fizz. You may fancy this a bit more than the straight stuff."

I took a sip, coughed, and sputtered when simultaneously the bubbles went up my nose and the liquid burned my throat.

"Right," he mumbled, taking the drink from my hand. "Let's try something a little tamer."

"It's fine. Really."

He unfastened his seat belt and walked the two rows to the front. When he returned a minute later with yet another bottle of liquor and a Coke, he proceeded to fill the glass with the soda, added a small amount of alcohol to it, and gave it to me.

"Thank you, um, sir."

When I took a sip, it tasted almost the same as what I'd had earlier without any alcohol in it. I set it on the tray, and he added more rum to it.

"Drink up. We're about to taxi for takeoff," he said, downing what was in his glass. He tossed it in the bag one of the other attendants held out to him. I did the same after guzzling what was mainly Coke.

"I'm Niven," he said, holding out his hand.

I shook it. "Harper, and thank you."

"Not at all."

I gripped the armrests as the plane gained speed, and squeezed my eyes shut. If Dave were with me, it would be his hand I held rather than part of my seat. I felt my cheeks heat, remembering how embarrassed I'd been when my stepmother burst into the anteroom where I'd been ensconced for what felt like hours. "I can't believe you were jilted at the altar," she'd exclaimed. That had earned her a glare from my mother, who asked her to leave so she could speak with me privately.

"I can't stand that woman," she'd muttered under her breath. Her sentiment didn't come as any surprise, given my father had left her for the "skeevy bitch."

"What will you do?" she'd asked.

"I'm going to London as planned."

My mother raised a brow.

"As Mouse said, it's paid for, so I should take the opportunity to travel."

She hadn't had much more to say on the subject. I knew she thought I wouldn't go through with it. Yet here I was, terrified I was making a huge mistake but at least proving her wrong.

2

Saint

I studied the woman in the seat beside me. She reminded me of someone, but I couldn't put my finger on exactly who. She was attractive-ish. Not my usual type. However, could I truly say I had one? I found most women beautiful in one way or another. This one, though, I found inexplicably intriguing. Given we had a little over seven hours to kill, I looked forward to getting to know her better. Anything to get my mind off the bloody events of the last few days.

Longer than that, if I were being honest.

It had been several weeks since I turned up at a meeting for a mission involving the extraction of a former CIA contractor to whom the Chinese government had given asylum.

Securing the invitation hadn't been easy since a few weeks before, I'd been sacked from MI6 for botching a different mission involving China. Once I was there, getting either of the units involved to add me to their team was even harder.

As I sat in on the meeting, I felt the disdain of my peers. I hadn't imagined it; their lack of respect was as heavy as it was thick.

I'd used the derision to convince the lead operative—Paxon "Irish" Warrick—to let me go along. It was a feeling he'd experienced for much longer than I had. For several months, he, like the man we would be extracting, was believed to be a double agent—a traitor—someone to be reviled, not just by those he worked with, but the entirety of the democratic world.

Begging as I had was not normally in my wheelhouse. At least not until then. My life had changed, though. I was no longer the *bon vivant* I'd once been. At thirty, I was young for a has-been, which meant a rebranding was in order.

If anyone in the espionage community were to ask about me, the first word likely to be used would be *lothario. Ineffective* would certainly be in the top three. *Former MI6 agent* would fill the remaining slot.

It wasn't just my professional reputation I needed to fix. What people thought of me personally was just as unflattering. What was I especially good at? Seducing women—à la James Bond—I'd heard frequently.

Perhaps when I set out to become a member of Her Majesty's Secret Intelligence Service, I'd fancied myself to be the real-life version of 007. I'd relied on my looks and charm throughout my life. Not doing so would be a difficult habit to break.

On the positive side of things, once the extraction had been successfully carried out—albeit with a minor gunshot wound to my right leg—I was one of the few people chosen to interrogate the man the Chinese called a "whistleblower" and everyone participating in the mission referred to as a bloody traitor.

It was one of the times being British served me, given the American's betrayal of his country was fueled by his hatred for it. Therefore, having a Brit question him instead of a Yank proved useful. That the Chinese had brought him to the brink of death when his "asylum" turned into detainment, made the man even more willing to give up the secrets we'd wanted him to.

When I was invited to the celebration of the last part of a yearslong mission, I saw it as a win. It took place two nights ago after the very man who'd given me a second chance, Irish Warrick, was given the Presidential Medal of Freedom.

While I'd sworn I would take it easy, the alcohol flowed freely at the gathering that had been arranged to take place in the hotel where most of us were staying. Thus, several of those assembled were more drunk than me. Not that being "less drunk" was something I could tout as an accomplishment.

I'd approached the bar to order what I promised myself would be my last drink when I noticed a woman—a stunning woman—sitting alone, her glass nearly empty.

"May I get you another?" I'd asked.

"Um, I said this would be my last." She lifted the drink that was now only ice.

"I've made myself the same promise," I said, motioning to the bartender. "One more, and then I'm cut off for the night."

"I guess I could have one more."

Three drinks later, for each of us, we were frantically tearing at one another's clothes in the lift that would take us to the top floor and my hotel room.

Like with my resolve not to overindulge, I vowed instead *tomorrow* I would curb my carnal excessiveness.

When I woke the next morning after very little sleep but hours of mind-blowing sex, I wasn't surprised to see my lover, whose name I couldn't recall, had sneaked out sometime between dawn, when we both passed out from exhaustion, and now.

I'd stretched my arms over my head, checked the time—a little after ten—and rolled out of bed. "One day at a time," I'd muttered to myself as I looked in the bathroom mirror at the man who looked far more like my father than the way I saw myself.

Two hours later, I'd walked onto the lift that would take me to the office of the newly named CIA director. Once there, I would request assistance in locating a Chinese national named Jinyan Tai Man. He was the son of a British diplomat and MI6 asset I'd been assigned to protect for the last two years.

Taking the mission on personally—since I hadn't yet been able to get support from either MI6 or the CIA—was yet another item on my path to redemption.

If I were to find Jinyan, who had been in hiding for almost a decade—and whom the US and the UK had great interest in questioning—maybe I'd be able to check "professional reputation improved" off my list.

I stepped out when the doors opened and, to my utter dismay, came face-to-face with the woman I'd shagged the night before. Repeatedly.

"Good afternoon," I said, approaching the less-stunning-than-I-recalled creature who had gone ghostly pale the moment our eyes met. "I'm Niven St. Thomas, and you are?"

Things hadn't improved from there. Director McTiernan—or "Money" as he was known to those of us who'd worked with him—exited his office just then. The man had not just an astronomical IQ, but also an uncanny sense when it came to picking up on nuances, particularly between members of the opposite sex. Not that he'd needed it in this case. That something inappropriate had happened between me and Ms. *Just One More Drink* was abundantly clear.

He'd stepped out of his office at the most inopportune moment to witness my exchange with his assistant, whose name I still hadn't learned.

When he motioned me into his office with a heavy sigh, I decided to change my tack and not even mention the mission I'd originally come to discuss. Instead, I thanked him for inviting me to the prior evening's celebration. I stood then and told him I'd be returning to England the next day.

So, here I was, on the first flight I was able to catch, and it had been on standby at that. I wondered if the woman seated beside me—Harper, she'd said—knew the person who had missed the flight, thus allowing me the last-minute seat.

I looked to where her hands still gripped the armrests. We were close to cruising altitude, and her eyes remained squeezed shut.

"You can let go now," I said, tapping the back of her left hand with my index finger.

She slowly opened her eyes and peered out the window. "I hate that part," she said, rolling her shoulders. "I actually hate all of it."

"Landings bother me more," I confessed.

"Why?"

I was about to launch into a diatribe about failed landing gear and fatigued pilots, but looking into her wide eyes, I refrained. Instead, I changed the subject.

"I don't suppose you know the bloke whose seat I managed to usurp?"

I instantly knew I would've been better off terrifying her with the dangers of crash landings. Her face tightened and turned red, and her eyes filled with tears.

"Bloody hell," I mumbled under my breath. "My apologies. I shouldn't have—"

"It's okay." She pulled a tissue out of her bag and blew her nose with all the grace of a baby elephant. While that might've turned most fellas off, it came to me then whom she reminded me of—Dr. Emerson Charles—the most beguiling woman I'd had the pleasure to get to know and my former boss' wife.

"My apologies," I repeated. "Fancy another drink?" I bloody well did. Rather than wait for her response, I stood and went to the galley.

"Well, hello again," said bottle-blonde, heavily made-up, overly perfumed Jane. One would've thought with all the physical embellishments, she might've spruced up the moniker a bit.

"Another round, if you'd be so kind. For myself and for the lady."

"Of course, sir," she responded a bit too abruptly. "My pleasure," she added with a saccharine smile.

I returned to my seat and set both drinks on the flat surface between the armrests. "I made a right mess of things, and I—"

Harper rested her hand on my arm. "Please don't apologize again. You've done nothing wrong. In fact, you've been really nice to me, considering I'm a blithering, emotional idiot who's also afraid of flying. You probably hoped you'd be sitting next to someone who had their nose buried in a book or was wearing earbuds and planned to sleep the whole flight. Instead, you won the jackpot when it came to the most annoying person to sit next to for seven hours."

I waited for a moment to see if she intended to continue. She took a long sip of her drink, sighed, and looked out the window.

"Harper—which is a brilliant name, by the way."

"Thanks. I don't even remember yours."

"Niven. However, most people call me Saint."

"Because you're so nice?"

I laughed. "On the contrary. Nice is not a word typically used to describe me. My last name is St. Thomas."

"Well, you've been very nice to me, and I appreciate it. In thanks, I promise to leave you alone for the rest of the flight."

"I wish you wouldn't."

"Pardon?"

"If you want to thank me, you'll do me the honor of allowing me to get to know you better, Miss…"

"Godfrey. Harper Godfrey. Although if my day had gone as planned, I would now be Mrs. David Lipscomb."

"Lipscomb over Godfrey? I'd say you dodged a bullet in the last-name department. So, what happened that you are traveling alone?"

She took a very long drink, almost emptying her glass, then shrugged. "He decided he didn't want to marry me."

"His profound loss."

"That's nice of you to say." Something about her downcast eyes and soft voice sent a surge of desire straight to my knob. Surely, this woman would bend to my will in a way no others had as of late.

"Why do I sense you were about to say 'but'?"

She smiled. "Maybe I'm the one who has suffered the profound loss."

"Absolutely not. You, Harper, deserve to be with a man who will hold you in the highest regard, love you endlessly, and make it his life's mission to do everything in his power to keep this lovely smile on your face." I was tempted to reach out and stroke my finger over her dimples.

So much for curbing my carnal reactions.

3

Harper

If there was any doubt in my mind as to whether I should've gotten on this plane, it was gone. The über sexy man sitting beside me was exactly what my ego needed after my morning's humiliation.

I'd carry the words he'd just spoken with me throughout what was supposed to be my honeymoon and probably long after I returned home.

He'd said I deserved to have a man hold me in the highest regard and to love me endlessly. I *did* deserve that. Dave clearly didn't feel either sentiment. Saint was also right about me dodging a bullet. Why would I want to spend my life with a man who would never make it his mission to keep a smile on my face?

"You're contemplating what I've just said to you."

"I am."

"And?"

"You're right."

"That was too easy."

"I'm not going to lie and say what he did doesn't hurt. It does. But is it more about the embarrassment I felt, or is it the pain of not having him in my life?"

"I'd say if you're asking that question, you already know the answer. How did you meet this… What did you say his name was?"

"My best friend calls him Douchey Dave."

Saint laughed out loud. "*Douchey* Dave. Brilliant. So, again, how did you meet?"

"In college."

"Where'd you go to university?"

"Belmont. It's in Nashville."

"Are you from Nashville? You don't have a Southern accent."

I shook my head. "DC."

"Ah."

There was something about the way he said the single-syllable word that seemed off. "Not your favorite place?"

He took a drink and gave a half smile. "Scene of my latest transgression. Tell me more about Nashville. Why there?"

His abrupt change of subject wasn't lost on me. "It was more about the university than where it was located."

"I recall Lipscomb having some connection to the city, although I have no idea what or why."

"Lipscomb University. Dave's third-great-grandfather founded it."

"That's where the douche went, then?"

I laughed at his use of Mouse's nickname for him and shook my head again. "He went to Belmont too. Lipscomb isn't at the same level."

"What was your major?"

I could feel my cheeks heat. When I told him, our conversation would probably come to an end. "Christian Leadership."

"Oh. Wow."

I looked out the plane's window. "That's most people's reaction."

"I didn't mean it in a bad way."

"Right," I murmured, too embarrassed to face him.

"Harper?"

"Yeah?"

"Please look at me."

I slowly turned my head.

"I didn't mean it in a bad way."

"Okay."

"I find it as fascinating as everything else I've learned about you thus far."

I laughed and rolled my eyes. "Yep, that's what they say about me. Utterly fascinating."

Saint's brow furrowed. "Why the self-deprecation rather than simply saying thank you?"

"You're right. I'm sorry. Thank you."

"Do you currently hold a job in Christian leadership?"

"No."

"May I ask why not?"

The truth was I'd become disillusioned with what I learned was the business of the church. Megachurches seemed to be everywhere, and they employed several ministers, each with their own specialty. Instead, I'd decided to go back to school, once Dave and I were married, and pursue a different degree. He'd been all for it. At least that was what he'd said. I wondered now if that was part of his reason for not wanting to marry me. Maybe he wanted a wife who worked and could help support the household. Or someone who was ready to start a family. "I'd rather not talk about it."

"I see."

"In fact, I'd rather not talk about me at all anymore. I'm sure you're far more interesting. If you're willing to tell me anything about yourself."

"I will do as soon as I've gotten us both a refill." He stood, but then sat back down. "On second thought, it appears they're about to serve dinner. A glass of wine might be a better idea."

I wasn't much of a drinker, which he'd probably already realized. And wine? Yuck. "I think I'll stick with water."

"Our choices are chicken, beef, or seafood. Which sounds best?"

I picked up the same menu card he held and read the descriptions for each. They all sounded so much better than I thought airline food would be. "Chicken?"

"Are you asking?"

I shrugged and he smiled.

"I'm enjoying you, Miss Godfrey."

"You're easily amused."

"Not at all, actually."

Saint convinced me to try a glass of Chardonnay with dinner, and I was surprised at how much I enjoyed it. He also offered me a taste of the salmon he'd ordered. When I told him I wasn't a big fish eater, he pressed me to take a bite, and that too, I had to admit, was fabulous.

He'd managed to keep the conversation all about me and nothing about him, but I was determined to switch things around.

"You mentioned DC was the scene of your latest 'transgression.'"

"You picked up on that, did you?"

I smiled, nodded, and took a bite of strawberry-covered cheesecake.

He folded his napkin, set it on the edge of his tray, and rested his head against his seat. "While many call me Saint, I can assure you I am anything but."

I kept my eyes on him and took another bite of cheesecake.

"You're an imp."

I shrugged a shoulder but maintained my gaze.

"Very well. Here goes."

I sat back in my seat and turned so my body was facing his.

"I am a bit of a rake, as they say."

Man slut was on the tip of my tongue to suggest, but given he was struggling with explaining his earlier comment, I kept quiet.

"One would think that one's personal life should be kept separate from their professional life, but given what I do, that hasn't been the case."

My mind raced with what it could be. Was his "wow" comment because he himself was with the clergy?

"What do you do?" I asked, dreading the answer.

"I was, formerly now, with SIS," he said in a quieter voice than he'd used to this point.

"SIS?"

He leaned closer and whispered, "Her Majesty's Secret Intelligence Service."

"Oh. Wow."

"That's most people's reaction," he said with a wink.

"Why is what you do off the job anyone's business?"

"My initial thoughts precisely. However, an email I received before our flight took off implies otherwise."

"Is that why you said, 'bugger me'?"

He chuckled. "You don't miss much, do you?"

"You *are* right next to me."

"The email I received was from my uncle, who has been newly appointed the UK's foreign secretary. In other words, the man my former boss' boss reports to."

"What did your uncle's email say?"

"He suggested that if I was willing to 'change my ways,' he might be able to pull some strings and arrange for me to be reinstated."

That sounded promising to me, and I said so.

"The thing is, since I was sacked, I've been working on doing just as he suggested."

"Was your transgression the reason you lost your job?"

He shook his head. "No, that happened weeks ago. Botched mission, as they say."

"What did you do, anyway? In DC, I mean."

"Let's just say that if you attend a work party and get pissed, err…drunk…make sure the woman you invite up to your room isn't the assistant of a high-ranking intelligence officer—one with the ability to sway my uncle's opinion about my worthiness."

"Surely, your uncle wouldn't have suggested being able to pull strings if he knew."

He took a deep breath and let it out slowly. "I fear it's only a matter of time."

"What do you think 'change your ways' means?"

"A personality transplant."

I smiled and put my hand on his arm. "What do you think it actually means?"

His eyes scrunched. "I suppose it means it's time to grow up."

4

Saint

Thoughts of this nature would typically turn me surly. And conversations were entirely out of the question. Except with two people. The first was Emerson, whom Harper almost immediately reminded me of.

I couldn't pinpoint exactly what it was about them I found similar. Maybe an underlying quirkiness. Or perhaps it was how easy it was to talk to either of them. I knew so little about my flight companion, yet I found I wanted to tell her things about myself I'd never told anyone.

"I think you would do quite well in the field of Christian leadership."

Her eyes opened wider. "What makes you say that?"

"You're quite easy to converse with."

Harper laughed. "You've told me one thing about yourself for every ten I've told you."

"But I find myself wanting to tell you more."

"Thank goodness."

This time I laughed. "Why?"

"I am literally the most boring person on this plane."

"No. You're absolutely not."

"Who else have you talked to?"

"Plain Jane, for one."

She cocked her head, and I motioned with mine.

"She's hardly plain," said Harper, eyeing the flight attendant who'd all but ignored her.

"You have more personality in your smallest finger than she possesses."

"She's very pretty."

"How would you know with all the batter?"

When Harper cocked her head again, I made a circular motion around my face.

"Oh. The makeup. Well, she does have a lot on."

"Whereas you aren't wearing any."

"I have a good reason."

I sighed. I'd stuck my foot in it. I had noticed her eyes fill with tears on at least one occasion. "Right. My apologies."

I looked from her deep brown eyes to the dimples that appeared when she gave even the slightest grin. Her long, wavy brown hair had been down when I first sat next to her. At some point, she'd put it up in a messy knot on top of her head. Periodically, she'd remove her round tortoiseshell glasses, almost as if to emphasize a point.

While the whole of her face was attractive enough, her features were far from perfect. Her nose was slightly too big, and her teeth were crooked enough that she should have worn braces. Her eyes were set a little too far apart, and the left was lazy. And yet, if I had to use one word to describe Harper Godfrey, it would be lovely.

It was impossible to guess her age other than I knew she'd graduated from university. Her porcelain skin showed no signs of age, and without makeup, she could easily pass for a teenager.

"How old are you?"

Harper's eyes opened wide a second time. "How old are you?"

"I'm thirty. Dirty, thirty, old man."

"Twenty-five. Barely alive." Her cheeks pinkened. "Meaning, I've barely started living."

"Understood—and appropriate."

Harper covered her mouth when she yawned and then stretched her arms over her head. Her waist looked small enough for me to almost wrap my hands around. Her arched back pushed her breasts forward in such a way that I couldn't stop myself from looking, leaving me feeling like a *very* dirty old man. I found everything about this woman delightful—and captivating.

"Would you please excuse me?" she asked, pointing to the aisle.

"Of course." I unfastened my seat belt and moved out of her way, surprised when she stood to her full height that she was taller than I'd expected. Maybe five feet seven or eight. She smiled at me over her shoulder as she walked toward the first-class lavatory, catching me checking out her perfectly perky arse.

I took my seat and pulled out my mobile when I saw Jane headed in my direction, hoping she'd take the hint and leave me alone.

I'd forgotten to connect to the plane's Wi-Fi earlier, did so now, and checked my email. Nothing pressing, and by pressing, I meant no rescinded offers from my uncle.

"Where are you staying in London?" I asked after I stood to allow Harper back into her seat and took mine beside her.

"The Savoy."

I wriggled my eyebrows. "Swanky."

"It was to be our honeymoon."

"Right." A fact I already found myself wishing to forget. "So, London? I must say it doesn't seem terribly romantic."

She shrugged one shoulder. "I didn't have much say in it."

"What?" I shook my head. "Yet another reason to bid good riddance to the dipshit."

"I'm surprised he didn't do what I did and go alone."

It became perfectly clear then why she was on this plane despite her fear of flying. She'd hoped he would show, and then perhaps they'd be reunited.

I was fortunate for more than just the open seat.

For the second time in just a few minutes, Harper covered her mouth and yawned.

"Get some sleep," I suggested.

"You wouldn't mind?"

"Why would I?"

"Right. Probably looking forward to the reprieve." She removed her glasses and tucked them into the seat pocket, angled herself so her back was to me, and covered herself with a pashmina.

I leaned close enough that my chest brushed her back. "Sleep well, Miss Godfrey," I whispered.

Two full hours later, I wished she'd wake up. Honestly, I'd wished that within minutes of her settling in. I'd attempted to sleep as well, to no avail, ordered another drink I'd had little of, and opened a book after making sure there were still no new emails from my uncle. After reading the same paragraph more than once, I closed the cover of my tablet and put it in the seat pocket in front of me.

When I glanced at Harper, like I had repeatedly, she was studying me. "Good rest?" I asked.

"Not really."

Did that mean she'd be closing her eyes once again, leaving me without her company even longer?

Her eyebrows scrunched. "What's wrong?"

"Why do you ask?"

"You're harrumphing."

I laughed. "Am I?"

She nodded.

"Truth be told, I missed your company."

She rolled her eyes but put up her pashmina and settled in for a chat.

All too soon, the pilot announced our descent.

5

Harper

While Saint had said he was no longer employed by MI6, he still carried some kind of credential that got us through customs in record time. At least that's what he'd said. I had no way of knowing how long something like that would normally have taken in a place as busy as Heathrow.

He insisted I allow him to take me to the hotel. An older man drove us, and when we arrived at the Savoy, Saint also insisted on coming in while I checked in. Maybe I was foolish to be so trusting of a man I'd just met, and on a plane no less. But there was something about him that made me feel safe. More, if it came down to it, I innately knew Saint would protect me.

Unlike my experience with customs, it seemed to be taking an inordinate amount of time for the man at the front desk to find me in the system.

"I'm terribly sorry, miss, but I can't find a reservation for either Godfrey or Lipscomb."

"I don't understand. I have a confirmation number."

He pounded away on the computer keyboard for several more minutes and sighed when Saint, who had excused himself to the gentlemen's room, returned and inquired about the holdup.

"As I've told Miss Lipscomb—"

"Godfrey," Saint and I said at the same time.

"Right. There is no reservation. From what I can find, it appears it was canceled more than two weeks ago."

"Two weeks?" The words hurt even worse than Mouse telling me Dave had changed his mind about getting married. If he canceled the hotel two weeks ago, he'd known then he had no intention of going through with our wedding.

"You have no rooms available?" Saint asked.

"Completely booked, as are most of the hotels this week."

"Understood." Saint led me away from the desk and over to a seating area. "I'm afraid—"

I put my hand on his arm. "I've already decided what I'll do."

He raised a brow. "You have?"

"It's easy. I'll take a cab back to the airport and go home. I shouldn't have come in the first place."

"That seems a bit extreme. I'm sure we can find some-place for you to stay so you can at least see London."

"I'd rather go home."

He sighed. "Very well, but let's make arrangements from here. You may not be able to catch a flight out until tomorrow."

I didn't know what I'd do if that was the case. However, trying to book a flight from here would be far easier than attempting to navigate an airport as big as Heathrow. I wouldn't even know where to begin.

I pulled out my laptop, connected to the public Wi-Fi, opened my email, and searched for my flight information.

"I don't understand," I mumbled when I logged into the airline's website and entered my confirmation number.

"What?"

"It says the reservation was for a one-way flight. It didn't say this earlier. I swear it didn't."

"Let me see." Saint took the laptop from my hands and tapped the keyboard. "It appears your return flight was canceled while you were en route."

"I can't believe this." I pulled out my wallet, trying my hardest to get through this without falling apart. "I'll just buy my own ticket home."

"No doubt it will be quite pricey at the last minute."

"No more expensive than staying on here a few more days."

"True."

He handed me back my computer, and I searched for the cheapest flight I could find. I hit the reserve button before I could talk myself out of it. I knew it would be a far cry from the first-class experience I'd just had, but I didn't care. I'd been foolish to get on the plane in the first place. The sooner I was back home, the sooner I could get on with the rest of my life—without Dave in it. Mouse had certainly been right when she called him douchey. Although right now, the words I'd use to describe him were far worse.

With every number of my credit card I entered in, I hit the keys harder. He had to have known I got on the plane, what was now, yesterday. Had he so little regard for me that he couldn't allow me a ticket home?

I entered my card's expiration date and security number and waited while the payment was processing.

I still had no idea what I'd do until flight time tomorrow, but I'd figure that out in a minute.

My laptop pinged, and a red message flashed on the screen. "Payment declined." As hard as I'd been hitting the keyboard, I'd probably entered the number wrong. But after I reentered it, the same thing happened.

"This can't be right." I logged into my credit card company's website to check my limit, which I knew was far more than the price of the ticket. "Available credit is zero?" I said, not intending to voice it out loud.

Saint took my laptop from my hands, closed the lid, and leaned it against the side of his chair.

"What are you doing?"

He took both my hands in his. "I fear you will find more that will be very upsetting. Rather than do this here, I'm taking you to my flat."

"But—"

"But nothing. Let's go, Harper." He picked up my computer, stuck it in its case, and tucked it under his arm. With the other hand, he grabbed my suitcase and walked toward the door. Once outside, he motioned for his driver to open the back and shoved my belongings inside before ushering me into the car.

"I don't understand what's happening," I said a few minutes into our silent drive.

"We'll be at the flat in a few minutes, and we'll talk then." He motioned to the man in the front seat, and I nodded.

"Where are we?" I asked when we pulled up in front of a crescent-shaped building that looked more like a hotel than a place where someone lived.

"My flat is on the top floor."

Saint got my bags, and his, out of the car, refusing to let me help him. I followed him in through doors that led to a lobby not unlike the one we'd been in at the hotel—except there was no visible front desk—and over to a bank of elevators. He seemed preoccupied, which made me feel worse about dumping more of my burdens on his shoulders. I just got the feeling that saying so wouldn't make it better.

Once in the elevator, he set the bag he'd been carrying in his right hand down and pressed his palm to a flat piece of glass. He left it there until we started to move.

The doors opened directly into a foyer where Saint dropped our bags.

"May I use the ladies' room?"

"Of course. My apologies." He showed me down a hallway. "First door on your right."

When I came out, he had poured two drinks, handed one to me, and motioned for me to be seated.

"I'm going to ask you a question that may seem intrusive."

"Go ahead."

"Did you and Lipscomb share financial accounts?"

"Not until recently."

"When specifically?"

What he was suggesting dawned on me, and my stomach sank. "A month ago."

He nodded. "Were your assets significant?"

"Not really. I had some savings—a small inheritance from my grandmother."

Saint leaned forward and placed his hand on top of mine, a look I couldn't quite decipher on his face. "I suspect you may find your credit cards maxed out and your funds withdrawn from the accounts."

The pit that had sunk my stomach was growing into a rock. As much as I didn't want to look to confirm his suspicions, I knew I had to.

When I stood to get my laptop, Saint reached out and grabbed my wrist. "You don't need to do this now."

"I do."

He nodded, stood, walked into another room, and returned seconds later. "Wi-Fi info," he said, handing me a piece of paper.

I murmured my thanks, hoping what Saint had suggested about the state of my finances was wrong, even though in my gut, I somehow knew he was right.

Sure enough, Dave had withdrawn almost every penny sometime yesterday. What in God's name would I do now?

My laptop slid to the floor with a thud. I put my head in my hands and cried.

6

Saint

I'd had no doubt I was right; however, it didn't make watching Harper confirm it any easier, especially when she dissolved into tears.

She wouldn't have much legal recourse, considering the accounts were likely in both her name and the bastard ex-fiancé's. There were other avenues that could be explored, though. Not that I would bring that up just yet. First, I needed to comfort her. But how without it being terribly awkward?

I hadn't known this woman more than twenty-four hours, and yet I wanted to wrap her in my arms and assure her that as bleak as things seemed, they would get better. I'd see to it they did.

The irony wasn't lost on me that my own set of woes, or the latest set, was due to my doing far more than wrapping my arms around a woman I'd known less time than Miss Godfrey.

"Harper?"

She moved her hands from her face, took off her glasses, wiped her tears, and stood. "I should, um, be going. I've already put you out."

I stood too and put my hands on her shoulders. "Is that what you'd accept if our situations were reversed?"

Her beautiful wide brown eyes looked into mine. "What do you mean?"

"If we'd met on a flight from London to the US, and once I arrived, I found I had no reservations and seemingly no money, would you wish me well and leave me on my own?"

"Of course I wouldn't!"

"Then, why would you assume that of me?"

She put her glasses back on and plopped down in her chair. "I'm sorry."

I walked out to the foyer, picked up her bag, and took it down the hallway to the first guest room. My flat was quite large by London standards, particularly given its location. There were four additional bedrooms, besides my own, if she found my first choice lacking.

However, I sensed Harper wouldn't utter a word regardless of her accommodations. I could put her up in the linen closet, and she'd not complain.

As it was getting close to noon, I wondered if she might be hungry. Not likely, given her news. I was famished, though, and went into the kitchen to see what Miss Bardwell may have left in the fridge. The woman had worked for my parents, and her mother had worked for my grandparents. I was here so seldom I didn't really need her, but kept her employed full-time anyway.

I was delighted to see she'd left a plate of fruit along with some cheeses and savories, which I took back out to the living room. Harper was standing by the window.

"Don't know about you, but I could use a bite to eat."

"Thanks," she murmured without looking over at me. "You have a beautiful view."

I grabbed a handful of grapes and stood beside her. "I'm fortunate that this flat has been passed down through my family."

She sighed. "You are fortunate."

"You haven't said much about your family."

"My parents are divorced. Dad left Mom for a much younger woman. Mom's bitter. Dad's indifferent. The stepmom isn't very nice."

I sighed like she had. "I see. Hence not my best attempt at conversation."

"You're fine."

"What would you fancy? Something to eat? A walk in the park? You can lie down, but I don't recommend it for jet lag."

"I honestly don't know. I've never been so unsure of…everything, in my life."

"A walk it is, then. The fresh air will no doubt do us both good after so long in the stuffy plane."

"I know this is very forward of me, but would it be an inconvenience if I showered first?"

"Certainly not. Come with me, and I'll show you to your quarters." I led her down the corridor to the room I'd chosen. "If this doesn't suit, there are others."

She surveyed the room. "It's lovely. Thank you."

"The lavatory is right through here. Private, as you can see." I motioned her to the en suite. "Closet is to the left."

"Oh. I, um, probably won't unpack." She looked away, but I saw her eyes fill with tears like they had so often in the brief time I'd known her.

The urge to gather her in my arms and guarantee I would see to it the dickwad paid dearly for what he'd done to her—as well as promising I'd look out for her while she was in London—was almost too strong for me to resist. I didn't act on it, though, knowing such declarations would make her more uncomfortable rather than less.

"Have your shower, and we'll take our walk."

I left her be and returned to the living room in time to hear my mobile ring. Rather than ignoring it, which would have been my druthers, I looked to see who was calling. My uncle. *Bollocks.*

"Nigel, what a pleasure to hear from you."

"I've just been informed of your return to England."

So much for niceties. "I arrived at the flat a short time ago."

"According to my secretary, you received my message but have yet to reply."

"I certainly intended to do so once I was settled."

"Interesting word choice, Niven. It's precisely the reason I rang."

As I'd anticipated, I thought but did not say. "Yes, sir."

"I've taken on the position of Foreign Secretary and, thus, oversee Her Majesty's Secret Intelligence Service."

As I was well aware by the countless times he'd mentioned it. I sighed, albeit inaudibly. The man, my mother's brother, had always been somewhat of a blowhard. "Yes, sir," I repeated.

"Bloody awful that you were sacked from your employ with MI6. That my own nephew is such an embarrassment does not sit well, given my new role."

"My sincerest apologies, Uncle." What would the wanker have me do that I wasn't already attempting on my own?

"We must rectify the situation."

Again, what would he have me do? While the next thing he said answered my question, it almost made me laugh out loud. Maniacally.

"You need to settle down, Niven, and what I mean by that is, it's time you married."

"Married?" I all but shrieked. "Nigel, you can't be serious."

"I am. What better way to illustrate how you've changed your ways? And not to one of those trollops you so often parade about with. Find yourself a nice young lady, nephew."

What was I to do? Pick one off the street? Someone dowdy perhaps? As much as I wanted my job back, I couldn't abide this. I was about to tell him just that when Harper came out of the bedroom.

What had he just said? Find myself a nice young lady? *Good God. No. I couldn't dream of it. Could I?*

"Nigel, I must ring you back later."

"This conversation isn't over, Niven."

"Not at all, Uncle." *Not at all.*

7

Harper

Saint looked downright pale. "Is everything okay?"

"Yes. Fine, fine. Ready for our walk?"

"Are you sure you still want to take one?"

"By all means." His abrupt tone jarred me. Whatever conversation I'd just inadvertently interrupted must have been important.

"I can go on my own if you need to resume your call."

"I'd like nothing less," he muttered. He shook his head and motioned to the door. "Let's get on with it."

His brusque tone set me on edge, shaking my already raw nerves even more. I just wanted to be home, curled up on my sofa under my fuzzy throw.

"I've changed my mind. I'd rather lie down." I didn't wait for his response, nor did I intend to lie down. Instead, I'd pack the few things I'd taken out of my suitcase and use the small amount of cash I had on me to get myself to the airport. Once there, I'd call my mother first, even though I doubted she'd have enough money for a last-minute plane ticket to get me home.

Worst-case scenario, I'd call my father. Given Dave had used up all my credit and taken all my money, surely my dad would help me return home.

"Harper?" My hand was on the bedroom doorknob, but the way Saint said my name, made me hesitate. I waited as he approached. "I'm sorry. As you may have gathered, my call was unpleasant. It's nothing to do with you."

Saint's annoyance, even if it was directed at the person he'd been speaking to, made me anxious. "I've inconvenienced you too much already. As I said before, I need to go home. There's no point staying on here any longer. I appreciate your hospitality so much, but I can't continue to impose."

"I wish you wouldn't go."

I studied him. "Why?"

He leaned against the wall and looked down at the floor. "I wish I could explain."

"Why can't you?"

His eyes met mine. "You'll think I've gone mad."

A pit formed in my stomach, a feeling I was getting far too accustomed to. Had I been wrong about him? Was I crazy for agreeing to come to his flat? He'd been nothing but a gentleman until now, but his demeanor since the phone call was so different.

"There's something about you. I just… Gawd, I sound daft even to myself. I don't know what to say other than I wish you wouldn't leave yet."

"Saint, I…" I stared into his sapphire-blue eyes. Was it my own pain I saw reflected in them, or was it his?

He sighed and ran his hand through his hair. "If that's what you really want, I'll make arrangements. However, I would really like the opportunity to show you around London. Prove to you that not all blokes are like the douchewaffle." He mumbled the last part, but I heard him.

I bit my bottom lip. Who was I that I was actually considering staying? At the very least, I should call my parents, shouldn't I? Or maybe just Mouse to let her know where I was, what had happened, and that I would be staying on here for another day or two until I could make arrangements to return to the States.

"I'll take a walk with you."

His smile was as unnerving as it was impossible not to mimic. He reached up and barely brushed my face with his finger. "I love seeing your dimples."

I blushed, looked down at the floor, and back up at him. The heat I saw in his eyes was entirely different than what had been in them a second ago. "Saint?"

He took my hand and led me out of the hallway. "Let's walk, then, shall we?"

"I've never seen anything like that," I said when we got in the elevator and he pressed his palm to the flat glass panel like he had before.

"Security in the building is quite elaborate, given it houses an embassy."

"Did you say an embassy?"

"Yes." He nodded. "Belgium. The US embassy was on the west side of the square, adjacent to this building, until a few years ago. Unsightly as it was."

Like before, the elevator didn't stop on any other floors before opening to the lobby.

"There's a lovely park right across the way. The same one you were admiring earlier."

When we walked across the street, Saint's hand occasionally brushed my lower back. I loved the feeling of it. How many times had I wished Dave would do something like that? Or even hold my hand. When I'd asked him about it, he said he found public displays of affection inappropriate. Now I wondered if there was something more to it. Maybe it was just public displays of affection with *me* he didn't care for.

We spent over an hour slowly making our way through the different parts of the garden. I found the memorial for those who lost their lives on September 11 particularly moving.

"Did your family know anyone?" I asked when Saint appeared introspective.

"They did."

When he didn't elaborate, I didn't ask any further questions.

"I'm quite famished," he said as we walked out of the gardens and crossed another street. I had no idea where we were or how far we'd gone from his flat. "Fancy a bite to eat?"

While I'd had no appetite earlier, I was surprisingly very hungry now. "I'd love it."

Saint chose a place with outdoor seating, stating it was a warm day by London standards.

"Anything sound good, or shall we share a few of the small plates?"

"Sharing sounds perfect. If you don't mind."

"Not at all."

I closed my eyes and turned my face toward the sun, happy to let Saint order when the waiter approached our table.

"What is this?" I asked when he returned a few minutes later and set a drink in front of me.

"It's called a Garibaldi Spritz. A bit of Campari, along with blood orange and cherry liqueurs, a dash of citrus sherbet, and a splash of prosecco."

I laughed. "I don't know what any of that is except the sherbet."

"Let me know if you like it."

I took a sip and groaned. "It's *so* good." Once again, the way he looked at me and smiled unnerved me.

"I knew you'd enjoy it."

"If the food you ordered is half as good, I'll be in heaven." As soon as I'd uttered the words, I felt silly. I'm sure Saint thought I was horribly unsophisticated. My cheeks flushed again, and I looked down at the peach-colored napkin on my lap.

"Harper?" When I looked up, Saint had leaned forward, his elbows on the table.

"Yes?"

"You are lovely." Evidently, he'd picked up on my insecurity.

"Thanks," I said, rolling my eyes. "I know I'm *unsophistified.*"

He cocked his head.

"A simpleton? Right off the farm? Or the plane, I suppose."

"You are none of those things." His gaze was so intense, I had to look away. When I did, he put his finger on my chin and turned my head toward him. "You are lovely," he repeated.

As much as I wanted to look away, I kept my eyes riveted to his. "Thank you."

"That's better." He sat back when the waiter approached with two plates.

"The beef carpaccio with shaved truffle and Parmesan and the peppered calamari, sir."

When Saint motioned in my direction, the waiter put a bit of each on the small plate in front of me.

"Bon appétit!" he said before walking away after Saint said he'd serve himself.

I'd had calamari before but had no idea what beef carpaccio was except that it looked like paper-thin slices of raw meat. I used one of the small forks to gently scoop a piece from the plate to my mouth. For the second time since we arrived at the restaurant, I groaned.

"Like it?" Saint asked, flashing one of his megawatt smiles.

"I'm not sure I want to know what it is, but it's *so* good." I was pretty sure I'd used the exact words to describe my drink. "I assure you, I do possess a better vocabulary. I graduated from college, after all."

"You're as delightful as you are beautiful."

Beautiful? He'd said I was lovely, but not beautiful. I closed my eyes momentarily and gave God a prayer of thanks. If there was ever a time in my life when I needed a handsome, charming, and terribly sophisticated man to tell me I was beautiful, today was the day. It did wonders to take away the sting of what Dave had done to me, even if only temporarily.

"Thank you." I looked down at my napkin for the second time.

My head snapped up when I heard Saint groan.

8

Saint

Every time Harper's cheeks flushed and she looked away, I was certain her intention wasn't to display submissiveness; nevertheless, my cock disagreed with my evaluation.

"What?" she asked with those wide, doe-like eyes that only served to make my trousers that much more uncomfortable. If there was ever any question of my rakishness, it was well illustrated now. How I wanted the young woman seated beside me in my bed, where I would pleasure her in ways she probably had no idea existed!

When she'd placed the slivered beef on her tongue moments ago, I was dizzy with the desire to feel it tangling with my own. More, to see her kneeling before me as my hardness eased between her lips. I had no doubt I'd be the first man to experience such a gift from her.

"Are you okay?" she asked when I wiped my brow with the handkerchief I'd removed from my pocket.

"Fine, fine. Quite warm out here on the terrace."

She nodded as if she accepted my excuse. "You'd never last in Nashville, especially in the summer. There were days when I couldn't bear the idea of putting clothes on."

"And what did you do instead?" I heard myself ask as though my brain had somehow gone off on its own with a very inappropriate line of questioning. Or perhaps it was my penis doing the talking.

She laughed. "Well, I *had* to get dressed. I could hardly parade around town naked."

I was in a serious muddle. I couldn't very well get up and leave the table, given the state of my straining zipper. A change of subject was in order, but I'd be damned if I could think of a single thing to say that would steer the course of this conversation in a better direction.

"I doubt my Christian leadership professors would have appreciated that."

And there it was. It was as though an ice-cold bath had landed in my lap. I breathed an audible sigh of relief when my trousers immediately felt looser. "No, I don't suppose that would've gone over."

The waiter returned with the other two dishes I'd ordered—sizzling shrimp served with warm ciabatta and oven-baked lobster with a chili-herb crust. I laughed, imagining my mother's look of dismay at the amount of seafood on the table. She'd never been the fan of it my father and I had been.

Thinking about my mum immediately reminded me of her brother, further casting a chill on the heat I'd felt moments ago.

Thus, I was able to finish our meal, along with dessert, without further carnal thoughts of Miss Godfrey.

"I don't think I can stay awake much longer," she said in the lift carrying us up to my flat. I checked the time and saw it was late enough in the day that going to bed now—sleep, not sex—wouldn't affect her as adversely as it would have earlier, and I said so.

"I should probably call Mouse first."

"Mouse?" I asked when the doors opened into the foyer of my flat.

"My best friend. Her name is Mary, but everyone has called her Mouse for as long as I can remember."

"What about you? What's your pet name?" Pet? God, what was bloody wrong with me?

"I don't have one. Harper was always odd enough that no one thought it was really my name. Some of the boys called me Harpo when they found out it was."

It was evident that the moniker bothered her. I found myself wanting to punish every person who'd hurt her—including the dickmonger. *Especially* him.

Which, if I gave in to my desires and seduced her, would be at the top of the list.

"Just *great*," she huffed.

"What?"

She held up her mobile. "No service. Could he really have shut my phone off?"

"Likely not," I assured her. "It's the building. I should've suggested you make the call while we were still outdoors." I followed her gaze to the window, where I saw it was raining. "You can use mine," I offered, pulling it from my trouser pocket and checking for any messages before handing it over to her.

"Are you sure?"

"By all means."

I kept myself busy in the kitchen, trying my hardest not to eavesdrop on Harper's conversation with her friend. Not that I didn't want to. Mainly, I wanted to know whether she was still planning to leave as soon as she could. I doubted it would be tonight, but tomorrow was a distinct possibility.

When she came out a few minutes later, I was seated with a circular open but hadn't read a single word.

"Um, you missed a call from someone named Cherry. Don't worry, I didn't answer. She may have sent a photo text too."

Whereas I'd seen her cheeks look flushed before, now they were burning red.

"My apologies," I muttered.

Harper turned on her heel. I waited until I heard the bedroom door close before looking at the image she'd obviously seen.

"Bloody hell." It could have been far worse, though. Instead of what I expected, Cherry had sent a relatively tame—for her—cleavage shot with a message reading, "Miss these?"

As I should've done long ago, I blocked her number. I didn't need to worry that she'd show up here. First, she'd never get past the lift's security. Second, Harper was the only woman who'd been in my flat, other than Miss Bardwell, since my mother passed away. Well, and Eliza, of course.

That was my rule. I never brought women home. If we couldn't have a shag at their place, there were plenty of London hotels that suited.

I walked down the corridor, knowing I owed Harper an apology but having no idea how to broach it. I was almost past her door when I heard her crying. I turned around and knocked softly.

"Yes? Just a minute."

I smiled when I heard her blow her nose and recalled how she'd done the same on the plane. The woman was maddeningly endearing.

She opened the door not much more than a crack.

"I wanted to apologize for the inappropriate message you witnessed."

"I tried not to look…"

"How could you not? Anyway, I'm sorry."

"You did warn me you were a rake."

"Yes, well, trying to mend those ways…" I gave her a self-deprecating grin. "How did the conversation turn out with your friend?"

She opened the door a bit more and walked over to the window. I took that as an invitation and followed.

"She wants to kill Dave, as you can imagine."

"A sentiment I share."

That appeared to surprise her, but she didn't comment.

"She asked when I planned to come home. I didn't want to tell her about the plane ticket. She can't afford to help me, but she'd try anyway."

"A good friend to you, then."

"The best."

"What did you tell her?"

"I said I wasn't sure, that I might do some sightseeing since I was already here."

"Does she know where you're staying?"

For the second time, her cheeks turned a bright shade of red, not as becoming as the pink I'd grown so fond of. "I didn't tell her the whole truth."

"No?"

"I said you were married and that you and your wife took me in."

"I see."

"I hope you're not angry."

"Not in the slightest. It will likely save me from being second on the list of people your friend intends to murder."

Harper smiled, exhibiting her adorable dimples.

"So. Sightseeing tomorrow? Where shall we start?"

"Oh! You don't have to show me around. I can go off on my own."

I shook my head and walked closer. "There is no way I'd consent to let you go off on your own, as you put it. While many areas in London are perfectly safe, some are not."

"I'm sure you have other things you need to be doing."

"Actually, I don't." I shrugged.

Her eyes widened. "That's right. I'm sorry. I forgot you lost your job."

"No need for you to be sorry. Although, a few days spent showing you the sights would definitely raise my spirits." I pretend-pouted, earning myself another of her smiles. "Will you allow me, then?"

"I don't know about a few days. Maybe one day."

I pouted again, and she rolled her eyes.

"Shall I plan an outing, then?"

Harper nodded. "If you wouldn't mind. I like it when you take charge. I mean, then, I don't have to think. I have so much on my mind, and I really don't know anything about London or flying or…anything."

I had no idea what my visible reaction might have been that caused her to so quickly backpedal, but I took it as my cue to leave her room before I did something I knew I'd regret—something like pulling her into my arms and kissing her.

I turned to leave. "Sleep well, Harper."

"Saint?"

I looked over my shoulder.

"Thank you for everything. You've been so kind to me. I honestly don't know what I would've done…" Her eyes filled with tears, and I was powerless to stop myself from embracing her.

"Shh." I took off her glasses, set them on the bed, and smoothed her hair. "I'm here, so there's no need to think about that." I pulled out my handkerchief but thought better of it since I'd used it to wipe my brow earlier.

Harper took a step back. "You're so kind. Too kind. Thank you."

I nodded, walked to the door, and wished her a good night for a second time before returning to the living room and pouring myself a finger of brandy. Once that was gone, I added two more.

Sleep would not come easy, knowing she was in bed only steps away. My God, she was beguiling.

"You are sorely tempting me," I muttered, looking up at the ceiling. "Is that what this is, or is it penance?"

9

Harper

I stood with my ear to the door, listening and wondering if, now that he'd said good night, Saint would return Cherry's call. It was ridiculous of me to hope he wouldn't. Beyond ridiculous, actually. I only prayed that when he did, he wouldn't invite her over. God, how horrible would it be to have to listen to him having sex? Especially since I hadn't. Ever.

The thought of that alone was enough to bring me back to tears. By now, I should've been a married woman, finally losing my virginity. Instead, I was in a stranger's home, in a foreign country, with no money besides the little bit of cash I'd brought with me. My credit cards were at their limit, I'd decided against calling my mother since she didn't have the means anyway, and I had no idea how my father would react when I called to ask him to loan me what I needed for a plane ticket home.

He'd probably force me to listen to a lecture about how I shouldn't have come in the first place. It wouldn't matter to him that when I made the decision, I thought I had plenty of money of my own, not to mention a round-trip ticket.

My dad had always liked Dave. In fact, there were times I thought he liked him more than me. I wondered how he'd react when he learned what my ex-fiancé had done. Perhaps I should reconsider asking my mother for the money.

Once I got back to the States, I could return to Nashville and the job I'd had, waitressing at one of the nicest restaurants in Twelve South, the city's hottest neighborhood. I'd made good tips there—enough that I could pay my mother back within a couple of months if that was the route I decided to take.

Of course that meant I'd have to try to get my room back, in the house I'd shared near the university. This late in the fall semester, there wouldn't be many people looking to rent rooms. By January, though, that would change. But for that, I'd need rent money.

I got in bed and stared up at the ceiling of Saint's amazing apartment, err, flat. Were they the same thing? He said he was fortunate that it had been handed down through his family, which must mean he owned it.

I wondered if I could get a job here in England. Was that even legal? If so, I'd be able to afford my own plane ticket home. On the other hand, where would I live? It was simply too much to think about. The first step, though, would be to look into whether a tourist could get a work permit. If anyone would know, Saint certainly would since he'd worked for MI6.

It seemed so unfair that he'd lost his job. Although he had said it was over a botched mission, not because he'd had sex with someone's assistant, I wondered if someone had an axe to grind against him.

I tossed and turned for what felt like several hours but was probably less than one. I hadn't heard any noise coming from outside the bedroom for quite a while, not that I could say exactly how long it had been. I sat up to look for a clock but didn't see one. I also didn't remember seeing a water glass in the bathroom.

Surely, Saint wouldn't mind if I went to the kitchen to get one. I tiptoed out of the room, being as quiet as I could so as not to disturb him, and went in the direction of a light that looked like it was coming from the kitchen.

"Harper?"

I nearly screamed when I heard Saint say my name. I spun around but didn't see him. "Where are you?"

"Over here."

I followed the sound of his voice. "Why are you sitting in the dark?"

"Why are you walking about my flat nearly naked?"

I looked down at the only thing I'd brought to sleep in. I'd planned to wear the lace nightie on my wedding night.

"I wanted a glass of water." Instead, I turned and started in the direction of the bedroom.

"You've forgotten something."

My eyes had adjusted to the light, and I could see him better now. He was seated in a chair. The dress shirt he'd been wearing was open, exposing his bare chest. He'd taken his shoes and socks off too and was slouched down, holding a glass in one hand.

"What?"

"Your glass of water?"

"I changed my mind. I'll be okay without it." Something felt off. Maybe I'd woken him. I was almost at the bedroom door when I heard him speak again.

"There's no need to be afraid of me, Harper." I hadn't realized he'd gotten up and was now so close to me that I could smell the liquor on his breath. "You know I wouldn't hurt you."

"You wouldn't?"

He looked up at the ceiling and shook his head before looking back at me. "Nor would I let anyone else do it. Never again." He maneuvered around me and opened a door across the hallway. "Fetch your water and get some sleep," he said before closing it behind him.

I woke the next morning to the sound of Saint talking to someone. A woman's voice answered. *Oh no.* Had *Cherry* come over last night after I went for a glass of water and returned to my room? I knew I'd fallen asleep minutes after that.

I got out of bed and went into the bathroom, where I could no longer hear them. After washing my face and brushing my teeth, I crawled back in bed. I slunk under the covers, wondering if I could get more sleep, when I heard a knock at the door.

"Miss Harper? Are you awake?" asked a woman whose voice sounded a lot like the cook on one of the British shows my mom liked to watch.

"I am."

"Mr. St. Thomas has asked that I prepare your breakfast whenever you're ready."

"Thanks. Um, I'll be out shortly."

"Take your time, dear."

I got dressed, put on a pair of shoes, and walked out to the kitchen. "Hello," I said, clearing my throat and hoping I wouldn't startle the woman since it didn't appear she'd heard me come in.

"Oh! Good morning."

"I'm sorry if I scared you."

"Not at all. Come in, come in." She motioned to the table. "You can eat in here or the dining room, whichever you'd prefer."

"I'll stay in here if you don't mind."

"Mind? I'd love the company. It's rare I'm not here on my own."

"Is, err, Mr. St. Thomas here?"

"He's gone to run an errand. He asked me to tell you he wouldn't be gone long." She dried her hands on a dish towel that was hanging from the waist of her apron. "Now, he said you might fancy coffee over tea. Was he right?"

"If it isn't any trouble."

"Trouble?" She responded like she had when I said I'd stay if she wouldn't mind. "Nothing's any trouble. Goodness knows I have a hard time keeping myself busy around here. One can only clean a room that's sat empty for months so many times. Niven, though, he'll never let me go, no matter how often I tell him I'm ready to retire."

I noted she hadn't referred to him as Mr. St. Thomas as she had earlier. She must have seen it on my face.

"Forgive my familiarity. I've known him since he was a wee boy."

"Please don't apologize for anything on my account. Can I help?" I asked, pointing to the stove, where something had started to smoke.

"Oh! The bacon!" She put a lid on the pan and moved it away from the heat. "Might be a little crisp," she said with a wink. "Fancy some eggs and toast?"

"If it's no trouble," I repeated.

The woman wiped her hands again and walked over to where I sat, and set a steaming cup of coffee in front of me. "Cream and sugar?"

"Just cream please. If it's no—"

She motioned to where it sat on the table. "That's the last time I want to hear anything about trouble."

"I'm sorry."

She patted my arm. "And no more apologizing. I've told you how happy I am to have company. Now, how do you like your eggs?"

"Sunny side up, please?"

"Same as Niven," she murmured, smiling as she walked back over to the stove.

"Ah, I see you and Miss Bardwell have gotten acquainted," said Saint, coming into the kitchen and startling me like I must have done to her. "Good morning," he said to me before walking over and kissing her cheek. "And good morning again to you."

"We're right chipper, aren't we?" She looked from me to him.

He sat in the chair next to me. "It's a beautiful day to explore London, isn't it?"

I looked out the window. "It does look like a beautiful day."

"I've all sorts of things for you to choose from." He fanned several touristy-looking brochures on the table and rubbed his hands together when Miss Bardwell set a plate in front of each of us.

"Wow. This is the best-looking bacon I've ever seen."

Miss Bardwell beamed. "I like her," she said to Saint before going back to get another plate. I thought perhaps she'd join us, but she set the dish of biscuits between Saint and me. "Enjoy your breakfast. I'll be off to make up your room."

"You don't have to—"

Saint put his hand on mine. "Let her. She's thrilled to have something to do."

"She said you won't let her retire." I grinned.

He laughed. "And if I did, she'd turn up here day after day anyway." The smile left his face, and he leaned closer to me. "My apologies for last night."

I rested my fork on the edge of my plate. "I know I'm an intrusion. I plan to talk to my father today—I sent him a quick message last night—and work out getting a ticket home."

His face fell, and he looked out the window. "I knew I'd made you uncomfortable. I'm such a bloody wanker."

I was making such a mess of this. I was the one who should be apologizing, not him. "You didn't make me uncomfortable." I waited for him to look at me, but he continued staring at something outside. "Saint?"

He slowly turned in my direction.

"You gave a perfect stranger a place to stay for the night. It was kind and generous of you."

"Perfect, yes. A stranger, no." He spoke the words so softly I could hardly hear him.

"I just can't take advantage of your hospitality any longer."

"What's this?" said Miss Bardwell, sweeping back into the kitchen. "I thought you said she'd be staying on?"

"What I said is that I *hoped* she'd be staying on."

The two of them looked at me. Did I dare think a man like Saint could be interested in me? Maybe it was just how hospitable he was that made me feel so much more comfortable than I ever did with Dave or his family.

"I feel like such a bother."

"You aren't. Not in the least. Is she?" The woman smacked Saint's arm.

"Couldn't be further from."

"See? Now finish your breakfast without any more talk of leaving." She topped off my coffee and left the room a second time.

"You're very kind—"

"You heard her. No more talk of leaving." Saint pointed to my plate. "Eat up."

Before I could take my dishes to the sink, Miss Bardwell swept back in and took them from my hands.

"I can—"

When she turned around and glared at me, I stopped talking. Saint pushed away from the table, stood, took my hand, and led me out of the kitchen. "It's a wonder she didn't smack *you*."

My eyes opened wide.

He laughed. "I'm kidding. She wouldn't have actually laid a hand on you."

"It kind of looked like she might."

"I'd never allow it."

I studied him when his tone turned serious. "Saint, I was kidding too."

"I meant what I said last night, Harper, about not allowing anyone to hurt you ever again." His gaze was so intent, so penetrating, I had to believe him, no matter how crazy it might seem.

Later, when I logged into my laptop and read the email my father sent, I prayed Saint truly did mean it.

10

Saint

Harper probably thought I was daft, but I meant every word I'd said about not allowing anyone to hurt her again, particularly the dumbfuck.

My main reason for going out earlier this morning was to get in touch with a man I knew would be able to track the whereabouts of her ex-boyfriend far faster than I could. Once tweedle dumber was located, the same man would ensure he returned every bit of Harper's money, even if it meant wringing it out of him.

If asked, I wouldn't be able to explain my fixation, perhaps obsession, with looking out for the young woman who had invaded my thoughts to the point I wondered if I had truly gone mad.

As I'd told Miss Bardwell, Harper was an innocent who had been heartbreakingly wronged. In fact, when she pressed me to tell the whole story, the woman I'd seen break down and cry only twice, when each of my parents died, shed a tear.

"Is it possible for someone who is visiting, to get a job in England?" Harper asked a couple of hours later as we walked the mile from my flat to Buckingham Palace, our first stop of the day.

"Are you asking for yourself?"

"Yes," she answered, cheeks pink, eyes downcast in that way that made me dizzy with desire.

"I'm afraid not. At least not in the regular sense."

She stopped walking. "What do you mean?"

"I suppose it might be possible to get a job as a nanny or perhaps a housekeeper of some kind that would pay off the books."

When Harper nodded and her tongue snaked from her mouth to lick her dry lips, I wanted to turn her into the alley we'd just passed and do it for her. Not just her lips. Her mouth, her neck, the breasts straining against her jumper. I closed my eyes and did what I'd done the night before to ease the ache I felt for her—I imagined Harper dressed as a vicar. And not a sexy one.

As we continued our walk, I scanned the surrounding area. It was a habit far too ingrained for me to ever change it. When the sunlight caught what appeared to be a camera lens, I quickly got on the other side of

Harper with my back to the guy to keep both of us from being photographed.

What in the bloody hell was that about anyway? While my family was prominent, the press had always respected my privacy due to my association with MI6. It was an unspoken rule I would soon speak up about if I saw it happening again. There was no way anyone outside the whole of SIS would have any way of knowing about my recent separation from the agency. Once an agent for Her Majesty, you were for life, regardless of employment status.

"Is everything okay?" Harper asked.

"Yes. Fine."

Her eyes met mine, and I wondered if she could read my mistruth so easily.

I discreetly nodded in the direction of the reflection I'd seen. "Paparazzi."

Her eyes opened wide.

"Not interested in us, I assure you. I'd just prefer not to be a photobomb." When her gaze penetrated mine, I shook my head. "Everything you're thinking is evident in your eyes."

Harper smiled. "What am I thinking?"

"You're wondering if I'm being forthright."

"Are you?"

I chuckled, put my arm around her shoulders, and pulled her close to me. "You are a delight, Miss Godfrey."

"Flattery will not distract me," she teased, but didn't pull away. Until she did, neither would I.

While Buckingham Palace was typically open to visitors from July to September, I'd made arrangements for a private tour anyway, so we were not limited to that which a normal tourist might be. Seeing the place I had frequented more times than I could remember through Harper's eyes was an unexpected pleasure. As I was learning, so many things were. She had an infectious childlike wonderment about her.

We were leaving the last of the King and Queen's State Rooms when the sound of my uncle's voice made me cringe.

"Niven? I'd heard you'd be visiting the palace today. I'm so happy I was able to catch you."

"Hello, Uncle. May I present Miss Harper Godfrey, a friend visiting from the States."

"A friend, you say?"

"It's very nice to meet you. Niven has spoken of you to me." Harper's manners put Nigel's to shame.

I couldn't help but look at her adoringly. "Miss Godfrey, this is my uncle, Nigel Fox."

When he studied her, Harper stood her ground, meeting his gaze in the same way she often did mine.

"What brings you to the UK, Miss Godfrey?"

I put my hand on the small of her back when her cheeks flushed. "She's considering relocation, and I offered to show her around."

His eyes scrunched. "What is your background?"

Harper's chin rose, and I knew better than to answer on her behalf a second time.

"I attended a Christian university, sir. I'd hoped to one day be a member of the clergy."

When my uncle looked from her to me, I found myself hoping beyond hope that he wouldn't disparage Harper in any way, particularly due to my sullied past.

"The clergy? Did I hear that correctly?"

Again, Harper spoke out before I could. "You did."

"Where? Here? In England?"

"It is my understanding that women have played an active role in the Anglican Church for more than thirty years."

Nigel cleared his throat. "While that may be true—"

"Your nephew has encouraged and supported me so kindly in my endeavor. It would be a dream come true to one day have a small parish of my own."

"In England?" Nigel repeated, appearing increasingly stunned.

Harper dropped her gaze in that way that made my every carnal desire roar to the forefront of both my brain and body.

"Yes. In England," she responded, looking up at me. I had no idea if that was truly a dream of hers she hadn't yet mentioned or if everything she said was for my uncle's benefit. Either way, I found myself proud of her.

"Perhaps you would both like to join your aunt and me for dinner."

"That would be very nice," Harper said before I could decline the invitation.

"I'll ring you later, Niven."

"Yes, sir."

"I look forward to getting to know your lady friend better," he said, effectively dismissing her.

I almost laughed out loud when I heard her say, "And I, you."

"This way," I said, motioning to the corridor that would lead out to the palace's gardens. Once we were a good distance from where we'd left my uncle, I stopped walking and folded my arms.

"Is something wrong?"

"That was quite a performance." I smiled and winked.

"That was the uncle who stands between you and getting your job back, wasn't it?"

"He is, you little minx."

"I didn't lie, Saint."

"You haven't mentioned an interest in pursuing a parish in our previous conversations."

"I didn't think of it until this morning."

"Are you serious, then?" Good God, she truly did want to be in ministry. And here I was, wishing I could pull her into my arms and kiss her, followed by ravishing her body the minute we returned to my flat. I doubted I was ever more ashamed of my inability to resist the opposite sex.

"It is merely one of endless possibilities," she responded with a wink.

"You understand that if I accept my uncle's invitation to dinner, you may find yourself answering a great many questions."

"I'll manage."

The smug look on her face told me she certainly would.

As we walked the two and a half miles of gravel paths that led us through the forty-two acres officially known as The Garden at Buckingham Palace, the conversations I'd had with my uncle over the course of the last few days rolled over in my mind.

It would be a logical assumption on his part that I'd paid heed to his suggestions and had found myself a "nice young lady." While Harper was that, I certainly hadn't gone in search of her.

When she'd walked from the hallway into the living room at the precise moment Nigel uttered those words, I had to admit, I momentarily considered our meeting fortuitous. If only to get Nigel off my back and working to get my job reinstated.

However, I'd immediately quashed the idea, knowing that using her in such a way would mean I was no better than her dookie of an ex.

I resolved to beg off the dinner with my mother's only brother and his wife, in fear the man would say something that would lead Harper to believe I was, in fact, using her.

That notion would be too easy for her to accept, given my inability to explain to her—or myself—why I was obsessed with her staying in London. One word from Nigel and the proverbial light bulb would go off, shortly followed by her returning to the States by any means possible.

"What's over there?" Harper asked, breaking me out of my reverie.

I looked to where she pointed. "Those are the Queen's private gardens." When I put my hand on the small of her back to walk in that direction, her breath hitched and her eyes met mine. "What is it?" I asked.

Her gaze dropped to the grass beneath our feet, and her cheeks pinkened. I put my fingers beneath her chin and raised her head. "When you do that…"

"Do what?"

"Put your hand on me," she whispered.

"Yes, well, when you look that way…"

"What about it?"

"It makes me want to…" God, I couldn't allow myself to say it. In the same way, I had to stop myself from envisioning Harper naked and spread out before me like a delectable feast.

The last thing she should do was exactly what she did. Harper took a step closer to me. Close enough that had it been any other woman, I would've reached out and encircled her hardened nipples with my fingertips.

"What does it make you want to do?" she asked in a voice so breathy I was tempted to lead her around the row of hedges that would shield us from the view of the public garden's other visitors, and suck all that breath out of her when I brought my lips to hers for the very first time.

I stared into her eyes, unable to stop my hand from cupping her cheek. "I've warned you I am a cad."

"Rake."

"Both."

"And?"

"Miss Godfrey, you test my resolve every time your cheeks blush the most beguiling shade of pink and you lower your gaze in a way that drives me mad. There is much about you that tempts me, but that in particular."

"I tempt you?" Her bourbon-and-Coke eyes, even shrouded by her glasses, drew me into their depths. When she absently worried her lower lip between her teeth, I found myself wanting its plumpness between mine instead.

"You have no idea," I said when her dimples appeared with her grin. "Or do you?"

"I don't know what you mean."

As I leaned further into her, Harper's quick intake of breath had my cock springing to full attention. God, how I'd love to taste those bee-stung lips. But if I did, I'd hardly be able to stop myself from whisking her to the flat, stripping us out of our clothes, and spending the next several hours—days—ravishing one another's bodies. While other women failed to hold my interest for more than a few rounds, somehow, I knew Harper would have it indefinitely.

I took a measured step back. "Shall we soldier on, as they say?"

Hurt radiated from her expressive eyes. I'd vowed to not let anyone cause her pain. Yet, in this case, I knew I was choosing the lesser level of it.

"Time for a bite to eat," I stated rather than asked. I took her hand and led her out of the gardens and across the way to one of my favorite spots.

While Harper had said she wasn't hungry before we were escorted to a table, when the restaurant's staff began bringing their Lebanese specialties without my having to order, she dove in with gusto. Once again, delighting me.

"I was intrigued by your interest in a vicarage," I said between bites of tabbouleh and baba ghanouj.

She smiled, perhaps for the first time since I'd summarily led her out of the palace gardens, warming me all over.

"While I would be interested in a vicarage if I were to become a vicar, I would have to complete my masters of theology degree before I was made the offer of a home." When I cocked my head, she continued. "A vicarage is a house, typically on church grounds, where the vicar resides."

"Ah. I see. I learned something new today. Although I would venture I will learn a great deal from you, Miss Godfrey. Would that I could keep you in London indefinitely."

When her cheeks flushed red rather than the pink I adored, I realized something must've occurred I wasn't aware of. Perhaps whatever it was, was the reason she'd asked me about the legality of her seeking employment.

"You can confide in me, Harper."

She turned her head when her eyes filled with tears.

"What's happened?"

"My dad…"

I leaned forward and covered her hand with mine. "What has he done?"

"It's more what he won't do."

"I see."

"You don't need to worry. You aren't stuck with me. I'll figure something out."

"I'll repeat. I'd keep you in London indefinitely if I could."

Harper rolled her eyes.

"Very well, to be more specific, there is nothing to 'figure out.' You are my guest, and you will remain such for as long as you'll allow me the pleasure of your company."

She shook her head. "You've been so kind. I can't take advantage of you any longer."

I took a deep breath and let it out slowly. "I've a confession."

"What?"

"I meant everything I've said about you staying on, Harper. The idea of you leaving fills me with inexplicable sadness."

She studied me like she had earlier.

"I'm being honest."

"I know," she murmured, nodding.

"You do?" I found her immediate acceptance flattering. "You have no idea the comfort you bring my soul." My words rang true as soon as I said them. "I do believe a role in the ministry is what you're meant to do with your life, Harper. I mean that sincerely."

Her cheeks flushed pink, but her gaze remained on mine. "Thank you, Saint. What about you? What is it you're meant to do with the rest of your life? Do you truly want to return to MI6?"

It came as no surprise that Harper would ask such a direct question. However, my lack of an immediate response stunned me. I put off answering by making sure my mouth was full of the delicious food that continually arrived at our table.

Finally, I sat back, toying with my napkin. "That you asked that particular question gave me pause. Do I truly want to return to MI6? I'm not certain. I suppose lacking any other direction in my professional life, yes."

"You said a botched mission resulted in losing your job."

"If only it were that simple. I suppose that was the straw that broke the camel's back, as they say."

"What happened?" She placed her fork down and leaned forward, giving me all her attention.

"I was tasked with providing detail for a man who was a known British diplomat. Not as well known was his status as an MI6 asset with strong ties to Hong Kong."

"How fascinating!"

I smiled at her sincere enthusiasm and lowered my voice. If we were going to continue this conversation, it would need to take place at my flat. "I don't know how much you pay attention to world politics, but any-one with ties to Hong Kong is either the sworn enemy of mainland China or they've figured out a way to use the takeover to their financial benefit." I looked at the rapidly filling tables around us. "What do you say we head out?"

Harper looked down at the food remaining on her plate and nodded. "I'm so full, I don't think I could eat another bite."

I motioned for the waiter, thanked him for taking such good care of us, and requested the bill. Moments later, the owner came to the table, and I stood. "Ahmad, it is so nice to see you. May I introduce my friend, Harper Godfrey?"

Rather than shake her extended hand, Ahmad kissed the back of it. "Welcome to my family's restaurant."

Harper complimented the food, and soon the two were in a lively conversation as she shared which were her favorites. I put my hand on his arm when he called for his son to bring more dishes to the table for her to try.

"While we appreciate your continued generosity, we will not be able to manage our way home if either of us eats another bite."

Both Harper and I thanked him when he insisted on packing up everything on our table for us to take with us, and on our way out, we promised to come back in a few days' time.

"What a nice man," she commented on our return walk to the flat.

"What a nice woman," I said, winking when she turned to look at me.

"I'm not sure how to say this."

"Go ahead."

"You have a very nice life, Saint. I mean, I know nothing of what it's like to work for MI6, but I would assume it isn't all pleasant. The rest of it, though, seems…"

I waited with bated breath, anxious to hear what she said next. I could almost assure her that whatever word or words she chose, she'd be wrong. Perfect, ideal, charmed, or even nice like she'd already said, would be so far from the actuality.

"Tranquil."

"Hmm."

"No?"

I draped an arm around Harper's shoulders, about to say one of the most honest things I ever had. "Lonely. At least until I met you."

11

Harper

The funny thing was, I could say the same. I'd never realized how lonely I felt before meeting him until he said the words.

I had friends in Nashville and at home in DC. Wait. Did I? Mouse, for sure, but was there anyone else I really considered a friend, or were they more acquaintances? None of my housemates even came to my non-wedding. That had been a relief, actually. It was bad enough to know I still had to tell everyone the wedding never took place. The humiliation I felt thinking about the people who'd sat in the pews, wondering what was going on, made me feel sick to my stomach.

Wait. Who *had* been sitting in the pews? I'd never looked. Had Dave's family and friends known and not shown up? I could ask Mouse or my mom, but I didn't want to know. If his side of the church had been empty, the only thing knowing would do would be make me feel worse.

I looked up at Saint, who was studying me.

"I'm sorry. I was just thinking how often I felt that way too."

"Lonely?"

"I heard a quote from a celebrity who said he'd once believed the worst thing in the world was to end up alone. He went on to say it wasn't. The worst thing was being with people who made him *feel* alone."

"And, as is said, money cannot buy happiness."

"It can only buy a plane ticket home," I said with a combination of regret and ambivalence. Was it wrong that as much as he said he wished I could stay, I wanted to equally?

"And that would not result in happiness for me."

"I wonder if it would for me, either," I responded, admitting the thoughts I'd just had.

Saint squeezed my shoulder with the arm that had been around me most of the walk back to his flat. "I suppose it makes me a right wanker if I attempt to assure you it wouldn't."

I shrugged. "Or it makes you nice enough to care whether it would or not."

He rubbed his chest with his free hand.

"What?"

"There you go again, soothing my soul."

We got on the lift, as Saint called it, and he pressed his palm against the flat panel as he'd done every other time. "I've never seen anyone else on this elevator or in this building. Other than Miss Bardwell, but that was in your flat."

"Not seeing anyone in the lift is easily enough explained, given it only goes one place. As far as not seeing anyone in the building, I can't comment, given I'm rarely here enough to notice."

Two things stunned me. He had an elevator all his own? Wow. As far as not being here, that made me understand his loneliness better.

Once inside the apartment, Saint put the food in the kitchen while I went to freshen up. There were things he and I needed to talk about, and I hoped we'd have the chance to. Mainly, I needed to tell him about my father's email.

I suppose I shouldn't have been surprised when I opened it and read that he had no intention of giving me the money to purchase a ticket home. Nor would he consider lending it to me. He'd gone on to say I'd proven my untrustworthiness through my actions.

At the time, I was too angry and hurt to think about much other than what I saw as my own father's betrayal.

Now, though, I couldn't help but draw the correlation between my situation and Saint's.

Other than getting on the plane and traveling to London, the circumstances related to my inability to get home weren't of my own making. The fact that Dave stole my money and canceled my flight seemed to be lost on my dad.

"I can hear you growling from the other room," I heard Saint say from the direction of the bedroom door.

"Sorry. Just thinking about what my ex did." When I came out of the bathroom and saw him standing in the doorway, I nearly gasped. The man was almost too handsome. Like a movie star. His hair, which had been slicked back when we left earlier in the day, had fallen forward. His eyes, always shockingly blue, sparkled when the afternoon sun streaming through the window shone on them. And his body? The man could've been a model with the way his clothes fit him as though they'd been custom made.

Maybe they were. Earlier, he'd said money couldn't buy happiness. I wouldn't be surprised if he were wildly wealthy. Only someone with a lot of money didn't appear to ever think about it.

"Still thinking about the ex?" he asked, jarring me out of my thoughts.

"Um. No."

"Glad to hear it, given the way your eyes have traversed down my body and back up again." He winked.

"You're very easy to look at."

"As are you."

I looked down at my sensible-for-travel clothes and rolled my eyes. "I'm a vision. That's for sure."

He strode in my direction, every step deliberate, until he stood close enough that I could feel his breath. I loved it when he did that. Even more so now since I didn't catch any scent of liquor.

"You are enchanting, Harper. That you are so unaware of it, only adds to the attraction."

When I felt my cheeks flush and cast my gaze downward, I heard Saint's quick intake of breath. I looked into his heated eyes and removed my glasses, wishing he'd act on whatever it was that affected him so.

"What does that make you want to do, Saint?"

"Do not further tempt me, Harper." He took a step back, and I took one forward. "I mean it. The rein I hold on my passions is tenuous."

"Let it go."

"You've no idea what you're saying."

"Then, show me."

Before I had a chance to even blink, Saint's mouth crushed against mine. His hand fisted my hair, and he angled his head to deepen his tongue's thrust into my mouth. Bone-melting heat spread throughout my body, and I leaned against him for support. The contact resulted in a moan that emanated from his chest and vibrated to the yearning between my legs.

I'd felt desire before, but nothing like this. The intense pressure made me want to grind myself against him, if only there was a place easily accessed enough for me to do it.

As if he'd sensed my building need, Saint backed me up against the wall and slid his muscular thigh between my legs. His hands cupped my bottom, and he tugged me against him.

My hands clung to his shoulders as I felt the intensity of where my clit ground against his thigh, building to the point where I was close to coming apart. I'd never felt something this strong. I wanted to climb his body and wrap myself around him.

"Harper." He said my name but nothing else, moving his mouth and lips fast, fierce, and oh, so demanding.

When I trailed one hand down his chest, he grabbed my wrist before my fingers reached his belt. I drew back and looked into his eyes.

"I'll let you take what you need, Harper, but I cannot give it to you."

"Why not?"

He released his grip on my butt and slid his thigh from between my legs. Whereas our bodies were plastered against each other's moments ago, now the only part of him touching me was his hands resting on my waist. "I will not—I cannot—take advantage of you."

"No matter how much I want you to?"

"Bloody hell," he whispered, bringing his forehead to mine. His lips trailed from my temple down my cheek. He nuzzled my ear, sending a new current of desire surging through my bloodstream. He lifted my sweater, pulled the cup of my bra out of his way, and circled my nipple with his fingertip.

"Oh, God," I groaned as my thighs clenched, desperate to feel his leg between them again.

"Hold on," he said. When his lips replaced his fingertips, my knees buckled.

"Please," I begged without knowing what for.

He moved his hand between my legs, cupping me in a way that felt so much better than his leg had. I held my breath as the base of his palm pressed hard against me. I gasped for air when a feeling like none I'd ever known ripped through my body. I cried out and buried my face against his chest as pleasure continued to course through me.

He withdrew his hand, brought his fingers to his nose, and inhaled. "God Almighty, you needed that."

I dropped my arms to my sides when I felt steady enough on my feet. "What about you? Don't you need something?" I stammered.

"Seeing you fall apart in my arms was all I needed, Harper. You've no idea the gift you've given me."

When he walked out of the room, the temperature seemed to drop by several degrees. I wanted to call after him, beg him to stay, beg him for more, but didn't, especially when I saw his shoulders droop slightly forward.

12

Saint

Never in my life had I wanted a woman more than Harper Godfrey. If I hadn't left her room, I would've lifted her into my arms, deposited her on the bed, torn the clothes from her body, spread her legs, and fastened my mouth to her slick, wet clit. I would've wrung climax after climax from her young, innocent body in ways I innately knew she'd never dreamed existed.

Her orgasm had shocked her enough that whatever suspicions I'd been harboring about her lack of experience were immediately confirmed. Harper had never climaxed from another's hand and likely hadn't from her own.

I walked over to the table where I kept the forever-full, thanks to Miss Bardwell, decanter of scotch and poured myself two fingers. I downed those and was about to pour another when I saw Harper out of the corner of my eye. "Fancy a glass?" I asked, picking up an empty tumbler.

"No, thank you. I'm really not much of a drinker." She walked over and sat in a chair near the fireplace. Her measured look had me setting the decanter down as well as my glass.

"I drink far too much." When she didn't say anything, my tentative smile laced with shame.

"Tell me more about the mission. I gathered it wasn't something we should talk about at the restaurant."

I was struck by her demeanor. It was as if my hand hadn't just cupped her pussy through her trousers, my lips hadn't just ravished hers. Rather than experience even more sexual frustration, I sat in the chair closest to her. "You were right. I shouldn't have said as much as I did."

She folded her hands on her lap.

"Where was I?" I said absentmindedly. "Dr. Adam Benjamin, I feel certain I didn't mention his name previously…"

"You didn't."

"Good. Right. Anyway, being assigned to him was definitely considered a slap on the wrist for me. The danger level, as well as the desired outcome, would typically mean a lower-level agent would be on the man's detail. However, since I was being given a second chance as it were, the duty fell on my shoulders." I wondered if Harper would ask what I'd done to garner the second chance. She didn't, but if she had, I'm not sure I would've been able to answer.

"Back to Benjamin. I traveled to the States with him for meetings he had scheduled with another expert on China policy, a woman named Dr. Emerson Charles. At the time, she was the leading authority on the subject at MIT's International think tank."

Studying Harper, I thought back on how, when I'd first met her on the plane, she reminded me so much of the woman I'd affectionately called Charlie but now knew as Emme. There were ways she still did, but now I saw *her*, not the woman who'd merely been an unrequited infatuation.

"Once in Cambridge, Dr. Benjamin made the suggestion that Dr. Charles be recruited as an MI6 asset on Chinese intelligence. My handler at the time—who is now Dr. Charles' husband—agreed to assign me that task."

Harper's eyebrows rose at my mention of my colleagues' marital status.

"That is an entirely different conversation." While I'd spoken the words, that I truly had every intention of sharing the story with her, stunned me.

Harper stood. "I'd like some water. Would you?"

I was about to stand to fetch it for her when she put her hand on my arm.

"I can get it."

I stayed put and allowed my gaze to linger on her backside when she walked away. I brought my hand to my face, closed my eyes, and inhaled her lingering scent. I'd not wash that hand as long as it remained, knowing it would too soon dissipate. The thought left me bereft. I adjusted my tightening trousers, getting myself repositioned before she reentered the room and handed a glass to me.

"I wasn't sure if you wanted ice. I prefer it without."

I took a sip and set it on the table beside me.

"I'm sorry I interrupted you. Please go on."

"It wasn't long before Adam—Dr. Benjamin—came to me, begging for my help with something I should've known better than to agree to."

I explained to Harper that the doctor had confided in me things MI6 had not been aware of. That we hadn't learned the information on our own should've served as warning the man was far wilier than he'd been given credit, but it didn't.

"He told me he'd had a long-term love affair with a woman named Jinyan Yanli. She was a Hong Kong law professor and activist who was also the mother of Adam's only child, a son, now an activist in his own right."

Harper sat forward in her chair. "I'm sorry to be so wide-eyed, but—wow—this is fascinating."

"What happened next was the beginning of the end for me. China had been negotiating heavily for Jinyan to be extradited back to the mainland to face criminal charges. Something the US, who had granted her asylum, was quite unwilling to do. Complicating matters was *her* desire to return."

"Why would she want to do that?"

"Two reasons. First, she was dying. Second, according to Dr. Benjamin, the Chinese were trying to make her believe they had her son in custody."

"But they didn't?"

I shook my head. What I'd done next was one of the stupidest decisions I made in my life. As I told Harper, I allowed Adam to convince me to go to Hong Kong with him.

"Once there, everything got exponentially worse. Almost immediately, we were picked up by the Chinese government and detained. As should've been expected, they then had plenty of leverage to negotiate an exchange."

"For Yanli?"

"That's right." I was surprised Harper remembered the woman's name, but I suppose I shouldn't have been. She had been listening with rapt attention.

"Was the deal made?"

I shook my head. "No, what happened was far worse for my career, but it did keep Benjamin from doing something rash."

Harper put her elbow on the chair's arm and rested her head on her hand. "*What happened?* Oh my gosh, I feel like I'm watching a movie."

"A joint US and UK team was sent in to extract us."

"In Hong Kong?"

"By that time, we were in China."

"Wow," she whispered.

I was glad she didn't ask for any further details since the extraction was anything but quick, easy, or efficient. In fact, one of the former MI5 agents who was part of the team had been shot in his right arm and came close to losing use of it.

"You asked why I was sacked. Mainly because I did the exact opposite of my orders and allowed Adam Benjamin to manipulate me into doing his bidding—something an MI6 agent learns not to do in basic training."

She nodded as if she understood, which didn't surprise me at all.

"The thing of it is, I came to look at Adam almost as a father figure. It's pitiful, really, but the man had a sadness about him that made me want to take care of him." I still wondered if the doctor had picked up on that and used it to ensure I'd do his bidding. "Anyway, to answer your direct question, that is why I lost my job."

"So, um, Saint. There's something I need to tell you too."

My first inclination was to get up and pour myself a drink. Instead, I took a sip of my water.

"I'm not sure how to say this, but after what happened earlier, I can't let this go on without being honest with you."

My hand gripped the glass more tightly as my urge for a drink grew stronger. What in bloody hell was Harper about to tell me? It sounded as though she was about to say she'd gotten back together with the dickbeater.

"Go on," I said through gritted teeth.

"I sent an email to my father—"

"You're leaving?" I couldn't bear to wait for her to cut to the chase.

"Actually, no."

"You're not leaving?"

"Not London, anyway. If you want me to find another place to stay, I suppose I'd leave then."

"Circle back to the email you sent to your father." I remembered her mentioning something earlier about my not being stuck with her. She'd been upset. Crying. "I take it your father has refused to fork over the money for your ticket home."

Her cheeks flushed red. "I'm mortified."

I stood and moved my chair closer to her. I sat back down, held her hands in mine, and took a deep breath. "Harper."

She smiled. "Saint."

"While I've said, time and again, that I would like nothing more than for you to stay on with me indefinitely, I will not keep you a prisoner. If what you truly want is to return home, I will purchase your ticket. No strings attached, as they say."

"Do you want me to leave?"

I rolled my eyes as she was so often prone to do. "I'm not certain there are more ways I could state otherwise, Miss Godfrey. However, for the last time, I *do not* want you to leave. I want you to stay. Not just in London, I want you to stay here at the flat, with me."

"Okay."

"Okay? I beg you to elaborate."

"I would like to stay."

I got to my feet, pulling her up with me. I gathered her in my arms in an embrace designed to convey my delight at her decision. However, her body was plastered against mine, flooding my mind with visions of what I wanted to do to her nakedness. Rather than act on my desires, I sat back down and indicated she should do the same.

"About what happened earlier." I'd seen Harper's face flush bright red on several occasions, but this time, it bordered on purple. I squeezed her hands. "Take a deep breath for me, Harper."

"If you're about to say—"

"How about if I actually say the words before you hear them?"

"I'm sorry. It's just that—"

"Harper." I furrowed my brow and used my sternest voice. "Let me speak."

She nodded.

"About what happened earlier, I want you to know that from this moment on—"

Her face was purple again, and it appeared she was about to cry.

"Bloody hell." I stood, but instead of pulling her up with me, I put my arms around her, lifted her from the chair, and carried her down the corridor to the bedroom I'd intended to suggest we retire to. Actually, I was going to suggest *she* retire there, and every word she'd feared I'd say had been on the tip of my tongue. Now, though, I couldn't possibly say I believed we should curtail any romance between us and remain just friends only so she didn't feel undue pressure. I wanted her to be comfortable here. Feel secure. It sounded as though few people in her life would provide such a respite for her.

When I rested her body on the bed and sat beside her, Harper turned her back to me.

"You don't need to say it. I get it, okay? I'm not exactly Cherry whatever her name is."

"You are nothing like her. You are—"

"A dolt."

"Hey, now." I tried to get her to turn toward me, but she refused to budge.

"Thank you for what you did for me earlier. As you said, I really needed it. Now, if you don't mind, I'd like to be alone."

This was going all sorts of wrong, but given Harper had interrupted me multiple times, I decided to do as she asked. Since she was staying on, there would be plenty of time for us to talk in the morning.

Rather than returning to the living room, where the first thing I'd do would be to pour myself a drink, I went into my bedroom and flopped down on the bed.

Today had not gone at all the way I imagined, and it was my fault it hadn't. The plain and simple truth was I couldn't be trusted around *any* woman, except perhaps Miss Bardwell. If she weren't like a grandmother to me, she'd likely be unsafe in my presence as well.

The fact that the first solution I came up with to the problem at hand was to scroll through the contacts in my phone was further proof that I was more the man my uncle believed me to be than the man I kept insisting I wanted to become.

13

Harper

I studied my tear-stained face in the mirror, wishing I was one of those people capable of keeping their emotions in check. I never had been, and it annoyed practically everyone in my life. Even my mom, who was twice as bad as me. It drove my father so crazy when I would tear up at the slightest thing, I once heard him say he wished he'd had a son instead.

Dave hated it too. Although, I'd say it would be a safe bet to assume Dave hated everything about me. I was a "mark" to him. Nothing more.

I pulled out my phone and calculated the time. It would be early afternoon in DC. Mouse might be at work, but that had never stopped me from calling before. Or her from calling me. I pressed her number and waited, remembering then that I couldn't get a signal inside Saint's apartment. I grabbed a jacket, toed on the shoes I'd just taken off, and slipped out of the bedroom door. I expected to find Saint in the living room, but he wasn't there or in the kitchen. I crept back down the hallway and was about to knock on his door to let him know I was going out to make a phone call.

"You've no idea how good it is to hear your voice," I heard him say. "Would that I could see you tonight, but I'm afraid I have a houseguest." There were several seconds of silence before I heard him add, "I'll do my best to get away tomorrow. Earlier in the day would be better, but I'll see if I can figure out a way to meet you for dinner. Soon, I promise." More silence. "Yes, luv, I miss you too."

As silently as possible, I tiptoed across the hall, eased open the bedroom door, and closed it behind me. Rather than risk bursting into tears where I might be heard, I went into the bathroom and turned on the shower.

I didn't cry, though, like I thought I would. I didn't know Saint well enough to shed tears because he had someone he loved. He'd said it himself. He wanted me to stay because he was lonely. Now that whoever the love was, was back in town, she could keep him company.

I took a deep breath, splashed cool water on my face, and reached in to turn off the shower. I needed to make a plan to leave. I wasn't foolish enough to go wander the streets of London alone tonight. Tomorrow, when he made up some excuse to go see his "love," I'd leave as soon as I was sure he was well on his way.

Desperate times, as they say, called for desperate measures. If my mom couldn't come up with the money for the plane ticket, I'd ask Mouse. If Mouse couldn't, I'd call my dad again, and this time, I'd beg.

After getting very little sleep, I waited until I heard both Saint's and Miss Bardwell's voices, then showered and stuffed what little I'd taken out into my suitcase, hoping I could figure out a way to get it out of the flat without her noticing. Worst-case scenario, I'd leave without it. Everything in it would either remind me of Douchey Dave or Saint anyway.

I lingered, hoping I'd hear the sound of the elevator or some other indication Saint had left. When enough time had passed that I realized he must be waiting for me before leaving, I rolled my shoulders, steeled my resolve, and opened the bedroom door.

When I saw Saint at the end of the hallway with his brow furrowed rather than in the kitchen, I worried I'd upset his morning.

"Everything all right?" he asked.

"I was about to ask you the same thing."

"Fine. Fine."

"You don't look fine."

"I considered knocking on your door or, worse, scanning the security footage. I worried you'd left in the night."

"Why?" *Oh, no.* Did he know I'd eavesdropped on his conversation?

He stepped closer and put his hands on my shoulders. "Because I'm such a bloody wanker. Because I continually do and say the wrong thing. Because I desperately want you to stay, and that alone should give you cause to escape under the cover of night."

"As if that would stop you from following her to the ends of the earth," Miss Bardwell said as she scooted past us toward the bedroom.

"Brilliant. That helps a great deal. Thanks ever so much," Saint drolled.

She chuckled and winked at me. "Good morning, miss."

"Good morning, Miss Bardwell."

Saint dropped his hands and smiled. "Anyway, good morning, Harper. I trust you slept well."

I was a terrible liar, even with something as mundane as how I slept. "Not really," I confessed.

Saint took my hand and led me out of the hallway entrance. "How about breakfast? Might that help? Maybe just coffee?"

"Sure. Thanks." I wriggled my hand free from his grasp and went in the direction of the kitchen with him following close enough that his palm rested on the small of my back. When we walked through the doorway, I gasped. The table was set with breakfast already plated. It looked as though it had been for some time.

"You didn't have to wait for me."

"I prefer your company."

If I hadn't eavesdropped on his conversation last night, I would've been flattered. Instead, I was annoyed. "What are your plans for the day? Or perhaps this evening?" I snapped.

His eyes scrunched. "I thought we'd discuss that over breakfast. I do have a couple of ideas that may interest you." He pulled out a chair and waited until I sat before taking the seat beside me.

"You don't have to entertain me, Saint. Please don't hesitate to do whatever you need to."

"Thank you for clearing that up for me, Miss Godfrey. May I ask what has you so surly this morning?"

I took a deep breath followed by a sip of coffee. "I'm wondering if there's someone else who might be able to help soothe your loneliness."

Saint raised a brow, but before he could speak, his cell phone rang. "Sorry, I've been expecting this call. Be right back." He stood and left the kitchen.

Moments later, I heard Miss Bardwell exclaim in delight but wasn't able to hear what Saint had said to her.

"You are in for a treat this morning," she said, whirling into the kitchen and putting a kettle on the stove.

"I am?" I said with less enthusiasm as I would have for a trip to the dentist.

"Yes, quite. Miss Eliza is in town and about to pay a visit."

"One of Saint's girlfriends, I presume," I said through gritted teeth.

Miss Bardwell laughed and walked over to rest her hand on my arm. "Not at all, but I do like seeing the fire jealousy brings to your eyes."

"I'm not jealous. I've no reason to be." I wasn't jealous at all. Not over a man I barely knew—no matter how nice he'd been to me.

"You've *every* reason. In the same way Niven was beside himself this morning, waiting for you to come out of the bedroom. I feared he'd wear a hole in the floor with his pacing."

We both stilled when we heard the elevator open followed by two voices.

"She's here!" squealed Miss Bardwell, racing out of the kitchen. Not knowing whether to follow, I stayed put.

I still wasn't certain if Eliza was one of Saint's previous love interests since all Miss Bardwell had said was that she wasn't one of his girlfriends. That didn't mean she hadn't been one in the past. As a mere houseguest, I wouldn't join them until Saint decided it was appropriate for me to do so.

"Where's Harper?" I heard Saint ask. I stood at the same time he rushed into the kitchen with a very beautiful woman in tow.

"Miss Godfrey, may I present Eliza Fox. Eliza, Harper."

"It is such a pleasure to meet you," the woman said, stepping forward. Rather than shake my outstretched hand, she embraced me and kissed both of my cheeks. "You were right," she said, turning to Saint. "She is lovely."

"Thank you," I murmured, lowering my gaze when I didn't know what else to say. Eliza, by contrast, was not lovely. She was gorgeous. In fact, she could very well be the female equivalent of Saint. "Wait. Are the two of you related?"

Saint stepped around the woman and put his arm around my shoulders. "My apologies. I should've said. Eliza is my cousin. My only cousin, in fact."

"I heard you had the pleasure of meeting my father," Eliza said, rolling her eyes. "My apologies if he said anything offensive. Which, clearly, he is prone to do."

"I'm attempting to beg off dinner with your parents for that very reason. However, now that you're in town, that may prove harder to do."

"I've a better idea. Let's plan a dine-out. That way, we can rest assured he won't cause a scene." Eliza turned to me. "We will also be sure to put Harper and him on opposite sides of the table."

I hadn't thought Saint's uncle—Eliza's father—was rude, but I'd take their word for it.

Saint squeezed my shoulders and kissed my temple. I expected him to drop his arm, but he didn't.

"I *love* seeing you this way," Eliza said, smiling indulgently at her cousin and me in a way that made me uncomfortable. Very uncomfortable. Saint and I hardly knew each other. Had he given her the impression otherwise?

"I'll just get you settled, then," said Miss Bardwell, who I hadn't noticed standing in the kitchen doorway.

"*We* will," said Saint, kissing my temple a second time before leaving the room with Miss Bardwell in tow.

Eliza plucked a piece of bacon off Saint's plate. "So, I hear you've an interest in becoming a vicar."

"Ministry of some sort. Yes. At least that's how I felt before the wedding."

Eliza's eyes opened wide.

"Wait. That isn't what I meant. I was *supposed* to be married, but my ex-fiancé decided he didn't want to go through with it. I'm not actually married."

She put her hand on her heart.

"What?" asked Saint, rejoining us.

"I thought you'd neglected to tell me you and Harper were wed."

"I was just saying that before the 'non-wedding,' I'd been reconsidering whether I would go into ministry."

Saint studied me. "Are you leaning against it now?"

I couldn't help but wonder why he'd ask, particularly with his cousin hanging on our every word. "I have many decisions to make before that one. My whole life to figure out, really."

Saint looked distracted but nodded before glancing at the table at my untouched meal. "Harper, you haven't eaten!" He pulled out my chair, and after I sat, pulled out the one he'd occupied previously for his cousin. "What about you, Eliza? Fancy some breakfast?"

"I ate on the train," she said, motioning for him to be seated. "Harper, I hope you don't mind my crashing here. I usually stay with Saint when I'm in town, so I can avoid the inquisition from Nigel and Millicent."

"Millicent is Eliza's mother," Saint explained as he took a seat and started eating the now-cold food.

"I am only a guest myself," I said when I noticed Eliza appeared to be waiting for my response.

"Very well, but if I'm a nuisance, don't hesitate to say so."

"I will not hesitate for even a moment," said Saint, winking at me.

"He's always been that way. Doesn't care at all about my feelings," Eliza teased before she leaned down and kissed Saint's cheek. "If you'll excuse me, I'll just go freshen up."

"My apologies. I had no idea Eliza was planning a visit until last night after you'd gone to bed," Saint said once his cousin had left the room.

"You don't need to apologize or explain. This is your house…err…flat."

He leaned forward. "I want you to be comfortable here." He took a breath as if he was going to say something more but shook his head.

"What?"

"Miss Bardwell said your bag is packed."

I knew my cheeks had turned red, and with the hurt look in his eyes, I knew I had to tell him the truth. "I overheard your conversation. I'm so sorry to have eavesdropped."

"My conversation?"

"Last night."

He looked as though he was trying to recall it.

"I heard you say you'd try to get away, and then you called the person you were talking to 'love.'"

"I see."

I felt so ashamed I was ready to rush out, grab my bag, and leave, just like I'd planned to. "I'm sorry." Before I could scoot my chair back and stand, I heard Saint say my name. It was barely above a whisper, but the emotion I heard in it made my heart hurt.

"Please understand, my cousin and I have always been close, given neither of us have siblings. When I called her 'luv,' it was simply a term of endearment." He took a deep breath and let it out slowly. "I know this makes no sense. I've thought about little else besides you and how the amount of time I spent thinking about you must make you feel. If I could explain it, I would. The closest I can get is to say I feel as though fate intervened the day of your wedding. While I cannot celebrate the pain and humiliation you felt nor the hurt and disappointment after discovering what your ex-fiancé did to you, I do believe that—for me—the stars aligned in the exact right order to put you directly in my path."

I took off my glasses and covered my face with my hands when my eyes filled with tears for the millionth time since I'd met Saint. No one, other than the man himself, had ever said anything so unbelievably sweet to me.

"I've done it again, haven't I?"

Instead of answering, I pushed back my chair and held my hand out to him. When he took it, I pulled him to his feet, put my arms around his waist, and rested my head on his chest. "Thank you."

"Harper?"

I turned my head to look at him but didn't stop there. I reached up and kissed him.

14

Saint

I didn't recall ever feeling such a profound sense of relief as I did when Harper, for the first time, embraced me of her own volition.

When she brought her lips to mine, I wanted to take control of the kiss, but stopped myself, allowing her to take the lead. When she pushed her tongue between my lips, I felt dizzy with desire but somehow managed to hold back. She pressed harder, thrusting her tongue deeper. I responded but with the rein on my passion held tightly.

When Harper's hand settled on my chest, right above my hammering heart, I wondered if she could feel how hard it was beating.

She put her opposite hand on my other pec and massaged the flesh beneath my shirt. When she leaned forward and kissed the skin just above my open collar, I lost hold of my control.

Burying my hand in her hair, I dragged her head up for a long, deep, hot kiss—one I never wanted to end.

It did, though, when my cousin returned to the kitchen and cleared her throat.

"I'd say I'm sorry for interrupting, but I'm not."

"You're a nuisance," I muttered, desperately wishing Harper and I had done more of this when we were alone. I'd been the governor of that accelerator, though, something I now regretted.

"I've been summoned. Evidently, my father's new position allows him access to the travel records of whomever he pleases. As he's aware I've arrived, I am now expected to join him for lunch. I'd apologize, but I somehow think you don't mind my leaving in the least."

I didn't, and I doubted Harper would either.

"Oh, and Miss Bardwell will walk me out."

The idea that in mere moments, I'd be alone with Harper left me breathless, particularly when I heard hers hitch. I closed my eyes, willing myself to exercise restraint, take things slow, treat her with all the gentleness, respect, and care she needed and deserved.

"Don't forget your appointment this afternoon," I heard Miss Bardwell holler from the other room. I had, in fact, forgotten entirely, and since it was more Harper's appointment than mine, I couldn't cancel.

I looked at the time. We had an hour before we had to leave. Too much and too little. Instead, we'd leave early and spend more time exploring the village we'd be visiting.

Once I was certain we were alone in the flat, I cupped Harper's cheek, put my arm around her waist, and pulled her body flush with mine.

"What appointment?" she asked as I nuzzled her neck.

"I've someone I want you to meet," I murmured before returning to my task of nibbling my way down the curve of her shoulder.

"Who?" Her voice was breathy with desire, making me wish I'd scheduled for tomorrow instead. However, I was lucky to get an appointment at all.

"It's a surprise."

Harper wriggled from my grasp. "Who?"

Noticing her furrowed brow made me feel terrible. The last thing she should be expected to accept without question was a surprise. She'd had too many of those over the past few days, none of them pleasant.

"I've arranged for a meeting with the vicar of a small parish in a village south of London. As he travels quite extensively, he didn't have many openings in his schedule."

Harper studied me. "Why?"

"I thought it might interest you. If it doesn't, I suppose I could—"

She stopped me talking by crushing her lips to mine. After kissing me soundly, Harper took a step back, cheeks pink and gaze lowered.

If not for the meeting with the vicar, I would not have been able to resist my desire to claim her.

"You're a very good kisser," she whispered, bringing her fingertips to her lips. "Lots of practice," she added under her breath.

Rather than argue, defend myself, or otherwise, I did as she had. I tugged her close, then took my time, nibbling her lower lip, softly brushing my lips against hers, tracing the outline of her mouth with my tongue, and finally, diving in with a promise of passion later— once we were back at the flat and alone.

I pulled away and rested my forehead against hers. "It isn't about being a good kisser; it's about who I'm sharing the kiss with. Like making love, whatever happens with our mouths, our lips, our tongues, isn't something I'm doing to you or you're doing to me. It's us coming together. I will never experience another kiss like the one we just shared, unless it is with you. And, Harper, *you* are an excellent kisser."

"You say the sweetest things."

"I don't. Not to anyone else anyway. Like so many other things, who I am with you…"

"Finish."

I smiled. "Who I am with you, Harper Godfrey, is the man I want to be."

"But it isn't the real you?"

"I can understand why you'd think that's what I meant. But it is the real me. I suppose you could say you bring out the best in me."

"I have a hard time believing you aren't this way with everyone."

Not that she'd asked, and I'd certainly never offer, but there were plenty of women who would vehemently argue that point.

The drive to Alfriston in East Sussex would take us just under two hours. Along the way, I imparted as much as I could recall about the historic village.

"It is an area rich in religious history, dating back to the year 1086. The clergy house"—I cleared my throat—"akin to a vicarage, was built in the fourteenth century."

Much in the same way she'd appeared fascinated by my story about Adam Benjamin, Harper looked transfixed. Especially so when I told her about the church we'd be visiting.

"It's said to be the smallest in England, although it is one of many claiming to be so. The vicar is responsible for, as he put it, the 'spiritual life' of a total of five small churches in the area."

"It's far closer to what I dreamed of when I first decided to go into the ministry. The idea of mega-churches is the reason I reconsidered my career path. I suppose that's why it was easy for me to tell your uncle I was considering a parish. The part about it being in England was a stretch, but whenever I closed my eyes and imagined my future, something small and quaint was what I always saw."

If I could influence her future, the part about a parish in England wouldn't be a stretch at all.

While I'd spent a good deal of time in the area known as South Downs when I was a lad, seeing it as I guessed Harper was, I was taken by the vividness of luscious green fields dotted with a herd of black-and-white cows drinking from a pond that appeared bright blue from the sky's reflection. The vast network of rolling mountains and the gorges and cliffs of chalk were something I'd explored endlessly. Based on her look of awe, I was sure Harper would enjoy walking the countless trails as much as I had. When did I stop making time to simply get out of London and breathe in fresh air?

While I'd anticipated we'd arrive early, our meeting with the Reverend Oliver Primrose was scheduled in a half hour. Rather than risk being late, I suggested we walk the grounds of the church.

As we exited the car, my senses were assaulted by the aroma of damp moss and wet tree trunks of the ancient wood, combined with the unmistakable smell of the salty sea. I breathed in deeply and allowed the memories of my childhood to remind me that life could be serene, peaceful, filled with hope.

It was no wonder so many writers made the South Downs region their home. The inspiration was endless.

"It's magical," I heard Harper say, perhaps more to herself than me.

I had to admit there was no more perfect word to describe the bucolic setting.

"Welcome," I heard someone call out, and turned to see the man I assumed to be the reverend approaching. Not that I would've known by his attire. He looked more like an English country gentleman dressed in tweed trousers, a dark olive-green waxed jacket with a brown corduroy collar, and Wellington boots.

"Miss Godfrey and Mr. St. Thomas, I presume?"

"That would be right. You must be Reverend Primrose."

After our introductions and a brief tour of the ancient grounds, I excused myself to allow Harper a private meeting with the vicar. "I won't be far off," I promised before kissing her cheek.

"Would be difficult to get far on foot in a place like Alfriston."

I tipped my cap that I'd donned after we got out of my 4x4, then went off in search of a very particular place.

I recognized the four-hundred-year-old cottage as soon as I rounded the corner onto the cobblestone road where Eliza and I first learned to ride bicycles.

It was my cousin who'd told me her father still owned it and had been renting it as a vacation destination up until the time he got the job as foreign secretary. Now, though, he was anxious to sell and was getting ready to put it on the market. When I asked if she wanted it, she assured me there was nothing she'd like less.

His selling, though, was an atrocity I could hardly bear. Had I put my flat on the market—even though I'd inherited it from my father's side of the family—there was no doubt Uncle Nigel would've added the "travesty" to my long list of disappointing behaviors.

While I couldn't gain access inside without alerting him, I walked around the perimeter of the property, astounded at how much of the garden I remembered. It was wild with brambles, weeds, and huge nettles, but beneath all that, I could see its beauty.

Once around back, where I couldn't be seen from the street, I traipsed through the thicket to peer in the windows at the large fireplaces and the wooden beams of the ceiling.

"Hello," I heard a woman's voice say. "May I help you?"

I backed out of the dense bushes, doing my best not to tear my trousers, and wiped my hands on my jacket. "I'm Niven St. Thomas," I said, extending my hand that I hoped was clean enough to not be off-putting.

"Niven, you say?"

"That's right."

"Niven!" She beamed. "I haven't seen you since you were a wee lad. I'm sure you don't remember me, but your parents and Miss Eliza's would leave the two of you in my care from time to time."

"My apologies that I do not. It's been many years since I've visited."

"What brings you round this way now?"

"I heard my uncle intends to sell."

The woman nodded, confirming it was common knowledge. "In fact, he's contacted my Barbara to handle the sale."

"Barbara?"

"My daughter. She lives right over there." The woman pointed across the way to another cottage. "There she is now."

A woman came out the front door and waved as she crossed the road and joined us.

"Barbara, dear, this is Niven St. Thomas."

"You don't say."

"Pleasure to meet you," I said, extending my hand to her like I had her mother.

"Again."

"Sorry?"

"You, Eliza, and I used to be thick as thieves. Of course, you were a couple of years younger than me then." The woman laughed heartily. "Still are, in fact."

I laughed. "Your mother tells me my uncle contacted you regarding handling the sale."

"He did, although there are repairs to be made before it can be listed."

"What's the asking price?"

"We've discussed eight hundred seventy-five thousand pounds, but it could be more."

"Is there somewhere we could talk privately?" I asked when I saw more of the neighbors assembling outside the gate.

"I've the key. Let's go in."

While we invited her to join us, Barbara's mother, whose name I hadn't gotten, said she'd deal with the "tourists," as she'd called them.

Once inside, I asked what the fair market value was for the cottage, added twenty thousand pounds, and requested she make an offer through a limited liability corporation I'd created several years prior.

She raised a brow but agreed to do as I asked.

Regardless of what did or did not happen in any other part of my life, mainly with Harper, I couldn't stand by and let the cottage go to anyone outside of our family.

"Are you back to London, then?" Barbara asked.

"Not certain. Think there's any room at one of the inns this evening?"

She handed me the key. "You can stay here."

"I don't want to get you in a fix with my uncle."

She laughed. "He'll be none the wiser. I manage it as a vacation rental too."

I checked the time and decided to head back to the church, given I'd have as much time as I would like to explore the cottage tonight.

15

Harper

"It's such a lovely chapel," I said when the vicar invited me to join him in the sanctuary.

"What is your first memory of a sacred place?"

"Easter when I was seven years old," I blurted. It was a memory so vivid, I didn't need to think about it.

"Tell me what you recall." He took a seat in a pew, and I sat beside him.

I closed my eyes. "I remember walking in the big red front doors that morning. It was still dark, but it was so bright inside. The entire area between the altar and the first pew was full of flowers. I didn't know what they were at the time, but the scent of lilies and hyacinths is something I'll never forget."

When I opened my eyes, his were closed. He was facing the altar, smiling. "Go on," he said.

I closed my eyes again. "I remember my grandmother held my hand and led me to the third pew from the front. I sat between her and my grandfather."

"Were your parents with you?"

"No. It was just the three of us."

"What else do you remember?"

"The joy." I felt a tear run down my cheek, but I wasn't sad. It was a beautiful memory. "The pipe organ. The choir singing. My grandmother's hand when she picked up the hymnal and showed me where to follow along."

"Anything else?"

"I remember the minister standing at the front of the church, with all the flowers behind him. The light from the sunrise streamed in the windows, casting a glow over him. I remember him saying Christ had died to save us from sin and that He had risen and was now in Heaven with God, His Father."

"Powerful memories for one so young."

"The most powerful."

When I opened my eyes, he was studying me. "Is that when you knew?"

I nodded, too moved to speak.

"While not of blessed Easter, my earliest memories are just as strong. I knew then, too."

"I lost my way," I confessed.

"It happens."

"I'm not sure why I'm here."

"But you sense there is a reason."

"I do."

"Will you pray with me?"

"I'd be honored." I took his hand and bowed my head. After several seconds of silence, I opened one eye and saw his still closed. He'd lifted his chin and was facing the altar. I realized then that we were praying together, but each with our own conversation with God.

"Amen," I heard him say moments after I did. "What did He have to say?" Reverend Primrose asked.

"I think this is where I'm supposed to be."

He smiled, closed his eyes, and nodded. "That's what He told me too."

We stood and walked the few steps to the back of the small church, where we discussed my education and what my plans were to further it.

"Am I interrupting?" Saint asked, walking up to us when we stepped outside.

"Not at all," said the reverend. "We'll speak again soon, yes?"

"Yes."

I watched him walk in the direction from which he'd come when he greeted us, knowing in my heart that I truly was where I was supposed to be.

"How did it go?" Saint asked.

"Significantly, and before you ask me to explain, I can't."

I expected him to press, but he didn't. "There's something I'd like to show you."

We drove the short distance from the church to one of the side streets of the small town that looked like an animated fairy tale brought to life. The cobblestone roads were narrow, but cars still tried to navigate it, coming at each other from both directions when it looked as though there was only room for one.

Charmingly crooked structures along the main thoroughfare housed shops and restaurants I longed to explore.

"What's this?" I asked when he turned off onto a side street, pulled up to the curb, and cut the engine.

"This cottage has been in my mother's family for several generations."

"Like your flat?"

"That was my father's family, but yes." He exited the car and walked around, opening my door. "Would you like to see inside?"

"I'd love to." Saint took my hand and led me through the garden gate. "Wait."

He stopped walking when I did. "Is everything okay?"

"I don't know who you are, Niven St. Thomas, or why you got on that airplane on the day I needed to meet you the most, but I'm so grateful you did. Thank you for bringing me here. Thank you for arranging for me to meet Reverend Primrose."

"You're welcome, Harper."

"And while I don't know why, exactly, you brought me here to this cottage, thank you for that too."

Like the town, the property resembled something from a fairy tale. I could envision the overgrown and unkept grounds restored to what had to have been the perfect English garden with rambling white rose bushes, hollyhocks of every color, peonies, and lavender. I could see herbs mixed in too—dill, rosemary, and catmint would be easy to tame from the sprawling mounds they'd become.

"I'm buying it."

"Wait. I thought you said it was in your mother's family."

"Yes. Uncle Nigel owns it."

"And he's making you *buy* it? That doesn't seem right."

"He did inherit, so by rights, it is his. Eliza is the one who told me he intended to sell. If anyone were to be put out, it should be her. However, she wants no part of it."

"But you do?"

"I've come to realize it, yes."

"Why?"

"I don't know. I suppose it's just a feeling."

I smiled. "I know exactly what you mean."

"You do?"

"I know this will sound crazy, but I belong here in…in…"

"Alfriston."

I laughed. "Right. In the town whose name I can't remember."

"If you wouldn't mind, I thought we might stay here tonight."

"I'd love that."

"Shall we go inside, then?"

While everything else felt so right, going inside now didn't. I couldn't explain either phenomenon; it was just something in my gut.

"Can we walk around first?"

I saw a flash of hurt in Saint's eyes, but he immediately hid it. "Of course."

"I'm kind of hungry."

"Good point. As am I."

Maybe that's what I was feeling in my gut. *Hunger.*

Saint and I ate at the Smuggler's Tavern, said to be Rudyard Kipling's inspiration for his poem, "A Smuggler's Song." Saint convinced me to try the roasted salmon, which was to die for, but I declined to taste the pork liver paté he ordered. "Maybe next time," I told him, which he didn't seem to buy. Wise man.

I nearly jumped from my chair when my cell phone rang. I'd gone so long without a signal while at Saint's flat, I'd forgotten to check once we left.

"Unknown number," I mumbled, deciding I should probably answer it anyway.

"Hello," I said at the same time Saint told me to wait.

"You fucking bitch. I'll get even with you for this."

"Who was it?" Saint asked when I dropped the phone on the table.

"I'm not sure." The call ended before I could respond, but the voice sounded like Dave's. Not exactly, but close. Something sounded off. "Maybe Dave."

"What did he say?"

I looked to the tables of people to our left and right. "I'd rather not repeat it, but I can tell you it's what I should've said to him, not him to me."

"Tell me, Harper."

"He called me a filthy name and then said he'd get even with me for 'this.'"

Saint nodded and pulled out his own cell phone. It appeared he sent someone a text.

"What's going on?"

"I'm trying to find out."

"Saint?"

"I asked a colleague to locate him."

"And?"

"I requested your assets be restored. I must say, I'm surprised it happened so quickly. Although I shouldn't be."

"My assets are restored?" While that news should've made me wildly happy, instead, I felt a sharp pain in my right temple.

"I can't say for certain." Saint studied me. "Are you all right?"

I took off my glasses and rubbed my eye. "It happens when I'm under a lot of stress."

"What does?"

"Pain. Here." I pointed.

"I'm sure the call from your ex was upsetting, but otherwise, if what I believe happened did, you should feel less stress, not more."

"I know."

"Has it been happening the whole time? Why didn't you say? God, again, a complete wanker. I've traipsed you all over, and the entire time, you've had a headache."

I held up my hand for him to stop, and put my glasses back on. How could Saint call himself a wanker? He'd been nothing but sweet to me. "First, it hasn't been happening the whole time. Second, if it had been, you would've known, just like you did when you asked if I was all right. Third, if I didn't want to 'traipse all over' with you, I wouldn't have." I rolled my shoulders. "Okay, now, back to my assets."

16

Saint

Absolute bloody bastard that I was, part of me wished it had taken longer for my colleague, Decker Ashford, to locate Dave the Dildo and get Harper's money back. The other part was happy for her.

Of course, this meant she'd likely ask we return to London tonight, and she'd be on a flight back to the States tomorrow.

As much as the idea of it left me feeling bereft, I should instead be grateful that I'd been able to spend any time at all with the lovely young woman sitting across from me. Wait. The same one scowling at me.

"Look. I'm pleased for you. I promise I am. Just give me a moment to feel sorry for myself, and then I'll be over it."

"What are you talking about?"

"You know what I'm talking about."

"I see. You're feeling sorry for yourself because you think now that I have money—*if* I have my money back—I'll go home." She drummed her fingers on the table as if she was waiting for me to respond. It didn't seem the statement warranted it.

"Uh, yes?"

"No."

"No?" Now my head was starting to throb.

"No, Saint. Think about it. Why would I go home?"

"Harper, my darling, forgive me, but I am simply not following."

"I have nothing at home. Nothing. Well, I have Mouse. She's my best friend, but she has her own life. Otherwise, *nada*."

"Nada?"

"Are you finished eating?"

I looked down at my nearly empty plate. "Yes?"

"Can we go back to the cottage and talk about this?"

"The cottage?"

"Are you going to continue repeating everything I say but as a question?"

I had been doing that, hadn't I?

More finger drumming.

"*No.* Absolutely not."

"I'd offer to get the check, but I'd rather wait to confirm whether I have money or not, so I don't embarrass myself."

Fingers. Drumming.

"Right. I should get the check so we can go." Rather than wait, I pushed back my chair and went to the bar to pay the tab. I was about to return to the table but saw Harper standing near the door.

"Are you sure you don't want to return to the flat?"

"Is that what you want to do?"

"No. Not at all."

Harper smiled and put her arm through mine. "Let's go back to the cottage, Saint. There's something I want to talk to you about."

Once inside the house, Harper used the lavatory while I rummaged in the kitchen, looking for a drink. Anything, really. Even vodka, which I detested, would do.

"Saint?"

"In here."

"What are you doing?"

"Looking for something containing alcohol."

"Come with me." She held out her hand, and I took it, resigning myself to the fact I would be forced to get through the conversation sober.

Harper sat on the sofa and pulled me down beside her. "Why are you assuming the worst? You haven't even heard what I'm thinking." After removing her glasses, she put her arm around my waist and rested her head on my shoulder. I immediately felt better.

"Thank you."

"You're welcome. Are you ready to listen now?"

"Yes."

Harper reiterated everything she'd said when we were at the tavern about there being nothing for her to go home to. She mentioned her best friend again, and how the woman had her own life. While she had a decent enough relationship with her mother, they weren't terribly close. And that her father had essentially left her high and dry in a foreign country meant she was considering whether or not to speak to him until he offered a contrite apology. Otherwise, she didn't have any other "relationships" worth returning to the States for.

"What will you do here?"

"I haven't told you about my conversation with Reverend Primrose."

My ears perked up.

"He's offered me a position as a curate."

I didn't want to go back to questioning every statement she made, so I waited for her to elaborate.

"His assistant." She smiled.

"Right. Thanks for the qualifier."

"The role will be unofficial for now, but as soon as he's able to make arrangements with the church to sponsor me in seminary, the status will change." She paused and looked into my eyes. "Any questions?"

"Endless."

She smiled. "As far as the seminary is concerned, I have two options. I can attend the University of Sussex or London Seminary. Once I've made the decision and have an official position of acceptance, I can apply for a student visa."

After asking around, I had learned the vicar was having a difficult time managing the parish that encompassed five churches, which is why I arranged for their meeting in the first place. However, I sensed there was more to his offer to help Harper than a desperate need for assistance.

When we left the church and they said their goodbyes, there was a visceral connection between them, and it pleased me immensely.

"I think the stabbing pain that came on at the restaurant was brought on by the idea that I would now be expected to go home."

"By whom?"

Harper raised a brow.

"Me? If so, please disregard that notion. I have already professed my desire to keep you in England indefinitely far too often."

"I need to make the decision about where to go to seminary."

"How can I help?"

"I'm glad you asked. We haven't known each other—"

"Stop right there. I've something I want to ask before you continue that line of thought."

Her brow furrowed. "Go ahead."

"Tell me about your interactions with the vicar." As curious as I was, I was also trying to prove a point.

"They were the same as my interactions with you, but very different too." Her cheeks pinkened, and she lowered her gaze.

I cleared my throat. "Exceedingly glad to hear."

"I get it, Saint, but what I'm going to ask isn't about a few days. I need to know that the decision I'm making is the right one for me for the time I'm at seminary."

"Ask."

"The vicar said the University of Sussex is about twenty minutes from Alfriston."

"And London is two hours."

"Yes."

"Here is what I suggest. We visit both, and any others worthy of consideration, and make the decision based on your comfort level."

"Saint, I don't expect—"

"I realize I interrupt you far too often, Harper, but there are times I find it too hard to bear the words I fear you're about to say. I want to do this. It isn't about obligation or merely being polite to a houseguest. I would be deeply disappointed if you didn't ask me to accompany you."

"I won't bring it up again, then. If the time comes when you don't have availability to be my personal escort around England, I trust you'll let me know."

"I will do."

"On that subject…"

I smiled. "Yes?"

"You said you wanted to beg off having dinner with your uncle, but isn't the idea to get him to help you get your job back?"

I'd given that subject a great deal of thought as I reacquainted myself with Alfriston. Did I want my job with MI6 back, or was it merely a means to an end that I didn't believe could be achieved any other way?

Ultimately, I wanted to be part of an independent team. There were three firms I would be interested in working with. The question was whether or not they'd have me.

My first choice would be the Invincible Intelligence and Security Group. They operated both out of Europe and the US. My former boss, Lennox "Lynx" Edgemon, the one married to my former crush, ran the Invincibles' East Coast headquarters near Boston. He'd likely be the hardest sell in agreeing to bring me on. Decker Ashford, the man I'd contacted to help find Harper's ex and get her money back, was a founding partner of the firm and ran the remaining US operations from his home in Texas.

In Europe, a man named Cortez "Rile" DeLéon was in charge. He had homes in both the UK and Spain. Of everyone on the Invincibles team, he was the one I was closest to. The man had an uncanny way about him that could be unnerving, yet his ability to seemingly know what I was about to say before I did, didn't bother me in the least.

As for the other two options, K19 Security Solutions was based entirely in the States. However, in my line of work, missions were global. The third, and smallest, was a start-up run by Wilder Whittaker and his wife and was based solely in the UK. From what I'd heard, they were known more for cyber security.

That I'd made a yet-unfulfilled vow to Adam Benjamin was my primary concern, over whether I was employed or not. He had agreed to not interfere in the US whistleblower's extraction, and in exchange, I had agreed to help him find his son.

My intention the morning after my "transgression" in DC had been to request the CIA's assistance in doing so. Knowing the intelligence the man could provide would be invaluable to the agency, I was prepared to make my pitch. After coming face-to-face with my prior night's one-night stand, I opted not to pursue the pitch. Looking back on it, my reasoning for abandoning the notion was based far more on my insecurity than my belief Money McTiernan would turn me down.

The question, then, wasn't whether I wanted my job back or not. The question was how best to fulfill my promise to Adam Benjamin. Given there was a long-standing manhunt, along with an attached bounty, both backed by the Chinese government, finding Jinyan Tai Man would be no easy feat.

However, with the help of the Invincibles team, I felt confident I could accomplish the mission. Whether Tai Man would want contact with his father after I did so, was something I needed to address with Dr. Benjamin before I got started.

There was also the question of funding the mission. If it came down to it, I could provide the financial backing myself in the same way I had with locating Harper's ex. Doing it at the same time I purchased the cottage from my uncle would put a strain on my port-folio but certainly wouldn't deplete it.

Harper tightened the grip she had around my waist, reminding me I hadn't answered her question.

"I'm considering a different approach."

"Something you want to talk about?"

At any other time of my life, the answer would be a resounding no, but everything felt different with Harper. As I shared my thoughts out loud, she remained fully engaged—interested—particularly when I spoke about my vow to Adam.

"You're a good man, Saint."

Her words were ones I hadn't heard often in my life. If ever. And I'd certainly never thought them about myself. It was easier to believe the bad stuff. Accept the negative as being ingrained in who I was. She saw the opposite in me and had since we met on the plane.

"Do they call you Saint because you're so nice?" she'd asked that day. I'd laughed. But now, knowing she believed it, made it easier for me to believe too.

"Fancy a walk before it gets dark?" I asked.

"I'd love it."

Round trip from the cottage to Cuckmere Haven and the Seven Sisters Cliffs was more than eight kilometers, so we opted for a shorter evening stroll along the Cuckmere River.

"The gardens are breathtaking," Harper commented as we walked past Alfriston's historic cottages.

"Those at Fox Run were equally beautiful at one time."

"Is that what you call your family's place?"

I nodded. "I'm sure they could be restored to their former glory without too much hard labor."

"I thought so myself when I first saw them. Do you enjoy gardening?"

"Honestly, I've never given it much thought." I stopped walking and took her hands in mine. "However, the pleasure I get from seeing your dimples is worth any effort it would require."

Cheeks pinked. Gaze dropped down. Cock hardened. Desire overwhelmed. It was an inevitable chain of events.

I grasped the back of Harper's neck and crushed my mouth to hers. I was momentarily worried she wouldn't want such a public display of affection in a town where she would be an assistant vicar. But when she wrapped her arms around my neck and ground the lower half of her body against mine, any thought, other than returning to the cottage and holding her naked in my arms, vanished.

"Can we head back now?" she asked, worrying her bottom lip between her teeth.

"I would like nothing more."

Fox Run Cottage was in view when Harper stopped walking. "Saint, how many bedrooms are there?"

"Four."

"Will you sleep across the hall from me tonight?"

"If that's what you desire."

"I do not."

I cupped her cheek with my palm. "What are you saying?"

"I want us to share a bedroom. A bed."

"What else, Harper?"

"I've never…you know."

I kissed each of her dimples, removed her glasses, and kissed each eyelid. From there, the tip of her nose and, finally, her lips.

"I want that with you, Saint. So much. Like everything else since we met, it feels right." She stared into my eyes. "Am I wrong?"

"Not even a little."

"It's more than a physical attraction. I know it is."

"It is so much more, my darling Harper."

"Do you want…me?"

"The fact that I am using your body to shield my body's reaction to you should tell you everything you need to know."

Harper looked down and giggled. "Should I apologize?"

"Never." I brought my lips to hers again, not that it would help the matter of our walking the rest of the way to the cottage without drawing attention. I didn't care. I couldn't stop myself. Kissing her had become like a drug to me. It was an addiction I never wanted to recover from.

17

Harper

There were a lot of reasons I was glad, grateful, relieved—hard to know which word fit best—that Dave had jilted me at the altar. None more than the fact I was still a virgin.

The one good thing I could say about the man I'd been supposed to marry, but didn't, was that he wanted to wait to have sex more than I did. Maybe it was his conscience that had stopped him each time I told him I was ready. Maybe not. Either way, we hadn't done it. We'd only kissed.

I liked what Saint had said when I told him he was a good kisser—no kiss of another would ever be the same as what we'd shared. It was one of the reasons I wanted him to be the first—pray, the only—man I made love with. Maybe he wouldn't consider it significant, but I would. No matter what happened between us in the future, I knew in my heart I'd never regret Saint being my first.

We stopped several times on the short walk to the cottage. Each kiss we shared was more passionate and unhurried than the one before it.

Once back inside, Saint stacked wood and lit the big fireplace in the living room. He took a blanket from the back of the sofa and spread it out on the floor, then tossed a few pillows on top of it. He held out his hand and pulled me into his arms.

A thousand butterflies fluttered in my stomach as he lowered me onto my back. "We're going to take this slow, Harper. There is no need for us to rush."

Whatever words I might have answered with were stuck in my throat as he trailed his fingers down the side of my face to my neck, where he'd moved my collar out of his way.

"I'm going to undress you now, my darling. Can you keep still while I do?"

I nodded. It was literally all I was capable of doing while he painstakingly unfastened the buttons of my blouse.

"We have all the time in the world," Saint murmured when I moaned.

I arched my back, wishing that instead of running his fingers down my sternum, he would touch my breasts that swelled to the point where my bra was snug.

"I told you to be still."

Before I could respond, Saint pulled the cup out of his way and gently bit the nipple of my right breast. I gasped in shock.

"Shh, now." He soothed the sting with his tongue. "Will you do as I say, or do you want to face more punishment, my darling?"

"I'll do as you say," I cried out when his hand cupped my pussy like it had the first time he brought me to an orgasm. "Anything you say."

"That's my good girl. Now where was I?" He made his way back up to my neck, nibbling on the taut muscles.

I nearly wept when his hand snaked around my back and he released the clasp of my bra. Once they were free of their confines, Saint lavished each of my heaving breasts with his tongue, lips, and fingers. I closed my eyes and breathed deeply, willing myself not to move.

When Saint grasped my wrist and moved my hand, I opened them. "The rule is, your hands must remain on your breasts. You can squeeze them, use your fingertips to play with your nipples, or circle the areola." He demonstrated each before lifting my left hand and placing it on the opposite breast. "Remember, Harper, your hands must remain where I put them."

I kept my hands still while Saint kissed a ring around my belly button and unfastened my pants. I gasped when I felt him reach inside my panties and cup my pussy the way he had before, but this time skin to skin.

"If you play with your nipples, I'll do the same here." When his finger touched the hard nub of my clitoris, I felt as though my body would levitate from the floor. I raised my head when he took his hand away.

"You know what to do, Harper."

I pinched both nipples between my fingers, and when I did, Saint put his fingers back on that magical place between my legs.

"Oh, my darling, you are so very wet for me."

When I groaned and squeezed my breasts together, I felt Saint lick my fingers and suck both nipples into his mouth. At the same time, he thrust one finger inside me, then two.

"I can't," I moaned. "Please. I have to move."

"Go ahead, Harper, take all the pleasure you want from my fingers."

I gyrated my hips and arched my back. The next sensation I felt was Saint's tongue, this time swirling around my clit. "That's it," I heard him coax. "Give it all to me." He licked and sucked as I cried out and writhed.

At some point, Saint carried me into the bedroom and finished undressing me. My eyes drifted closed.

"Harper," I heard him whisper. "Keep your eyes on me."

He unfastened his shirt, exposing the hard outline of his abs. He shrugged it from his shoulders, removed his belt, and lowered his trousers.

In awe, I watched as he strode toward me and stopped at the side of the bed. When I sat up, he spread my legs and stood between them.

"Can I touch you?"

"Do you remember what I did to you?"

I nodded and stared up into his eyes. "I do."

"Use your mouth, Harper. Your hands too. Do whatever you think will feel good."

I held him with both hands and swirled my tongue around the tip of his penis. Based on his groans and the way his fingers threaded in my hair, I knew I must be doing something right. Every so often, he'd hold me still and move his hips where he wanted my mouth to be.

He eased away, releasing my hands and mouth, and pushed me on the bed. With his hands on my waist, he moved me so my back rested on the pillows and positioned himself between my legs. He took a breast in each hand and massaged them.

"What we are about to do will hurt, Harper, but not for long. I promise."

18

Saint

"I trust you. Completely."

The power of her words surged through me; I felt their importance somewhere deep in my soul. Since I met her, I'd innately known I wanted to be the kind of man Harper would say those words to. She trusted that even though what I was about to do would bring her pain, I would also ease it, and then make her forget it entirely. Her cries would only be of pleasure.

With her beautiful wide eyes, she watched as I sheathed myself with a condom, spread her legs, and swirled her clit with the tip of my cock like I had with my fingers. Her wet heat beckoned me, and I could no longer resist.

I slowly eased inside her, my movements slight, as her eyes stayed riveted to mine.

"More," she begged, but nothing would make me rush this. I wanted to savor the feeling of being the first man to join my body with hers.

Harper gasped and gripped my arms as I went deeper. When she stilled, I did the same, waiting until I felt the gentle movement of her hips, her body's way of telling me she was ready for more. Her fingernails dug into my skin, and I brought my mouth to hers, thrusting my tongue between her lips in the same way my cock thrust into her pussy.

"Harper," I groaned. I held her hips with both hands, buried my head in her neck, and found our perfect rhythm.

When I felt her clench, I raised my head. I had to see her face, look into her eyes, not miss a single moment of Harper climaxing for the first time with me inside her. I could feel it building, but couldn't wait. I reached between our bodies, and before I could do more than touch her clit with the tip of my finger, she cried out, gasping for air, her body bucking against mine as I continued to thrust deeper and deeper.

"Ride it out, my darling," I told her when her eyes pleaded with me. "You can take more, Harper." I squeezed her hardened nub between two fingers, sucked her nipple into my mouth, and increased my pace. The moment I knew Harper had climaxed again, I let myself join her.

As I lay with my head resting on her beating heart, Harper trailed her fingertips down my arm and across my back.

"That was…"

I raised my head to look at her.

"Otherworldly. We danced among the moon and stars. It was as though they swirled around us. There were fireworks too. Shooting off like the grand finale on the Fourth of July."

I shifted my body so I could reach her lips and kissed her. Never in my life could I have dreamed there would be such a beautiful description of lovemaking. Nor one more perfect.

Harper and I spent all night learning each other's bodies. I marveled at her sensual awareness and thanked the stars that swirled around us whenever we brought our bodies to the height of pleasure, that I had been the only one to experience being with such a unique and special woman.

When I asked whether she'd like to spend the next day visiting Sussex, she begged that we spend the day together, alone at the cottage. A request I was more than happy to oblige.

"I've been thinking about your friend Dr. Benjamin," she began as we sat at the table in the kitchen, eating the baked eggplant with spinach and chickpeas and Thai green curry I'd had delivered from the tavern. Little by little, Harper was getting more adventurous with the food she was willing to try. "We never finished that conversation."

"I suppose I'll figure it out eventually." I brought her fingers to my lips and kissed their tips.

She put her elbow on the table and rested her head in her hand. "Or we could talk about it now."

I smiled. "There are things I'd rather do than talk."

"We can do those after."

"Very well, Miss Godfrey. I'm anxious to hear what you have to say on the matter, given your relentlessness." I thought I caught a glimpse of an eye roll.

"If I said I would *eventually* figure out what I planned to do with the next few months of my life, I doubt your response would be that much different than mine."

"Touché."

"Anyway, if you were to try to find the doctor's son, how would you get started?"

"I suppose first I would need to have a sit-down with Adam to see how much he actually knows about Jinyan's possible whereabouts."

"After that?" When she put a forkful of food into her mouth, I recognized it as the same ploy she'd utilized on the plane in order to get me to talk and not turn the conversation around to her. Minx that she was.

"Once I feel confident the mission is viable, the next step would be to assemble a team."

Harper nodded and took another bite.

When I didn't say anything else, she rested her fork on the edge of her plate. "Where is your friend now?"

"Meaning Dr. Benjamin?"

"Yes."

"I'm not entirely certain, but if I had to venture a guess, I'd say he's likely in London."

"A visit with him could correspond with one to London Seminary."

I grinned and shook my head. "Perhaps I should ring him, then."

"Perhaps you should."

The enthusiasm Adam displayed when I inquired about meeting made me feel worse about putting him off as long as I had. Initially, he'd suggested tomorrow.

However, I wasn't willing to give up the time I had alone at Fox Run with Harper so soon.

We settled on early next week, which would give me time to finalize the paperwork for the cottage's purchase, as well as arrange for Harper's visit to the University of Sussex.

"Do you need to meet with the vicar today?" I asked after ending my call.

"No, not until I make a decision about which seminary I'd like to attend." She worried her bottom lip.

"What else?"

"I've been thinking about Dave's call."

"Come," I said, holding out my hand.

She motioned to our unfinished meal. "I need to clean up."

"We'll get to that. We aren't going far." While Harper must've assumed I was whisking her back to the bedroom—which I gladly would as soon as I could—I led her only as far as the living room.

Once we were seated, I pulled her into my arms. "Tell me what you're worried about."

She let out a deep breath. "While you were on the phone, I checked my balances. There is more money in the account than was there before, and I saw Dave's name had been removed from it. The same with my credit cards. They're paid in full and only in my name."

Nothing she'd said was news to me. "Do you have a question?"

"Some of that money is his."

I shook my head. "Consider it compensation for your inconvenience."

"I don't feel right about that."

"Very well. Tell me what you'd like done, and I'll ensure it happens."

"I want all but five thousand dollars returned to him."

"Is that the amount you had in savings?"

"I had more, but I should help with the costs associated with the wedding being canceled."

While I understood Harper's position, I disagreed that she should help pay for a wedding the doofus called off. Before I could say so, she spoke again.

"I also think I should give him money for my flight to London."

These decisions weren't mine to make, but the amount she was considering giving back to him made me angry. I wanted to refuse to help her with any part of refunding Dave, but could I deny this woman anything? I doubted it. Perhaps her parents or the friend with the rodent nickname could convince her she didn't owe the dimwit one iota of reimbursement for costs he'd incurred himself. Not to mention, he'd left her penniless and stranded in a foreign country. I meant what I'd said about compensation for her inconvenience. I shuddered to think what may have happened to her if I hadn't gotten on that plane.

"Before you do anything, I strongly suggest you consider discussing it with someone other than me." I caressed her cheek when I saw she was worrying her bottom lip again.

"If I call my mom or my dad…" She shook her head.

"What about your friend?"

"Mouse? She'd tell me not to give him anything. In fact, she'd probably tell me to use the money to hire a hit man."

Something told me the best friend and I would get on quite well.

"Let's set that aside for a bit and circle back to the vicar. You mentioned your role as his assistant would be unofficial 'for now.' Did he give any indication when he'd like you to start?"

"As soon as I can."

"What's involved?"

Harper's cheeks flushed my favorite shade of pink, but given we were talking about the vicar, I tried my damnedest not to think about sliding my hand under her blouse and toying with her nipples.

"He's suggesting I assist with services here in Alfriston, primarily. Once I feel comfortable with that, I would take on another of the small churches."

Delight shone in her eyes; I leaned forward and kissed one of her dimples. When she turned her head, I did the same to the other.

"I should put the food away," she murmured moments before I covered her lips with mine.

"Leave it." I gathered her in my arms and carried her into the bedroom, where I intended to make Harper my dessert.

On Saturday, Harper and I attended the morning service at the historic chapel. The vicar introduced her to the handful of residents in attendance, suggesting that with her assistance, services could go back to being held on Sundays. That alone appeared to endear her to the congregation.

Part of me hoped my presence wouldn't incite God's ire, given I couldn't recall a time in my life when my family had attended a Sunday morning service—or any other day of the week. There had been weddings and funerals, of course, but otherwise, I'd never warmed a pew.

In my line of work, there were many occasions when I'd prayed to a higher power either for myself or my teammates. I'd no idea what that power's position was on taking another's life, even when deemed *necessary.* I only hoped that the deity Harper so strongly believed in was benevolent when it came to me.

At the service's conclusion, we stayed behind to chat while the vicar offered his apologies for rushing off to another of the five churches in his parish.

A number of the questions from the people gathered were addressed to me. I did, however, manage to steer the conversation back to Harper.

When one of the women invited us to join her family for lunch, I quickly mentioned our plans to visit Cuckmere Haven and the Seven Sisters Cliffs that afternoon. We had no such plans, but Harper's quick acceptance and thanks for the reminder told me I was right to ward off an afternoon spent with one of the parishioners. If word got around we had, Harper would be expected to visit all of their homes.

"Thanks for helping me dodge that bullet," she said as we walked from the church to the cottage.

"I vow to protect you from any and all bullets, whether literal or metaphoric."

Harper tucked her arm in mine. "Hard to believe it was only one week ago I was supposed to be married."

I couldn't help but wonder if she considered that dodging a bullet as well. I certainly did.

"It seems so much longer, doesn't it?"

"A lifetime."

"Do you mind?" she asked, pointing to a bench on the edge of the path.

"Not at all." We sat side by side, nodding at the people who walked by, sometimes saying hello, but otherwise, neither of us spoke. When we decided to, we both did at once.

"Go ahead," I said.

Harper studied me. "I believe I was supposed to meet you, Saint. I thought perhaps I was supposed to meet Reverend Primrose too, but now I disagree. It was you who led me to him. The moment you got on the plane in DC, the course of my life was altered. Does my saying that make you uncomfortable?"

"Not in the least." I draped my arm around her shoulders. "Have you considered that perhaps it was *I* who was supposed to meet you?"

"Maybe it was mutual. What were you going to say?"

"Oh, uh, I've forgotten."

"No, you haven't."

She was right. I was too ashamed to admit I had been about to ask if she actually wanted to visit the Seven Sisters or skip that and spend the afternoon in bed.

Harper rested her head on my shoulder. "Would it be okay with you if we didn't go on our walk?"

I almost laughed out loud. "I'm happy to do whatever you'd prefer."

"Can we go back to the cottage?"

"Of course. What would you like to do once we arrive?"

Harper didn't need words to respond. I knew she'd been thinking the same thing I was when her cheeks turned pink and she cast her gaze downward.

19

Harper

I wondered if most people had sex as much as Saint and I did. It seemed doubtful since we spent the better part of every day and night in bed.

Truly, it didn't matter to me whether it was excessive. I couldn't get enough of Saint's naked body next to mine.

"You know what to do," he said, closing the front door behind us. Need pooled between my legs from those words alone.

"I have particular desires I believe you will enjoy," he'd said after I gave him my virginity. "When we are together, alone like this, I want you to do as I ask."

Even then, before I had any idea what he meant, I knew I'd do whatever Saint told me to do. I suppose I should've worried what that might entail, but I didn't.

"You were made for this," he said now, as I removed my clothes, folded them, and placed the stack in his arms. Saint deposited it on the coffee table but appeared to change his mind as he walked toward the hall.

While I stood silently, hands clasped behind my back, waiting for him to tell me what to do next, Saint went into the bedroom. When he returned, he set one pillow on the coffee table and another on the sofa.

"I considered having you on your knees, but I've changed my mind."

My eyes followed his movements as he spread a blanket on the same table he'd set the pillow.

"Here, Harper." He pointed. "I want you on your back with your legs spread."

If he didn't know already, soon he'd be able to see evidence of how much I wanted this.

I got on the table, rested my head on the pillow, and was about to spread my legs when he did it for me.

"Keep your eyes on me, darling." He stood where I could see him and removed his shirt. "Touch yourself, Harper. Both hands." I knew where he meant.

I gasped when my finger skimmed over my swollen clit, hardly able to stand how good it felt. I wanted to give in to my body's need to writhe, but I knew better. When he was like this, Saint wanted me still.

Once as naked as I was, Saint knelt at the end of the table, took ahold of each side of the blanket, and pulled me toward him so my pussy was almost hanging off the edge.

I knew better than to move my hands, even when I felt his tongue snake between my fingers.

"Hands above your head," he said, positioning my legs over his shoulders. My knees trembled when his tongue swirled my clit and he eased two fingers inside me.

My head moved from side to side as the pressure building inside me came to a crashing halt when Saint moved his mouth away and nipped the inside of my thigh.

"Let me hear you, my darling." When the moans I'd been holding in escaped my lips, he dove back in, mouth and hands. A climax ripped through my body, and my eyes met his. I knew he'd be watching me; he always did, even with his mouth attached to my pussy.

"Saint," I whimpered, moaning his name. I watched him roll on a condom, pick up the pillow from the sofa, and tuck it under my bottom. He lifted my legs so they were around his waist and entered me in one thrust. His fingers dug into the fleshy cheeks of my ass as he picked up his pace.

"Harper," he groaned. I opened my eyes and stared into his. He stilled, and I could feel him pulsing inside me. Our eyes continued to bore into each other's until he finally pulled out, gathered me in his arms, and carried my sated body into the bedroom.

I closed my eyes momentarily when he went into the bathroom to get rid of the condom. I opened them when I heard his footsteps returning, in time to see him put on another.

"I'm just getting started," he said when my eyes opened wide and I smiled. I wasn't at all surprised. Saint could keep this up for hours, us taking turns pleasuring each other, until all we had the strength for was sleep.

Saint arranged for us to spend two more weeks on our own at Fox Run Cottage. We'd visited the University of Sussex, which was certainly in the running. While not as welcoming as a place like Belmont University, its close proximity to Alfriston made it worth considering.

After putting Dr. Benjamin off three times, I finally talked Saint into returning to London the following week, using the excuse that I needed to visit that seminary and make a final decision.

Citing a delay in closing escrow on the cottage and wanting to get on with it, he agreed.

I understood his reluctance to leave Alfriston. Being here with him was like a dream. It wasn't just the sex between us that was so amazing. Saint and I could spend hours talking too. I'd talked more to him in three weeks than I did to Dave in all the years I knew him.

Or didn't know him. He certainly hadn't known me.

I could talk to Saint about my fear and insecurity in wanting to pursue a life in ministry, and though I doubted he knew much about the life of a vicar, he appeared interested. Even enthusiastically reassuring me that it was a job meant for me.

In turn, he spoke at length about his life as an MI6 agent and whether he wanted to return to it.

We'd finally gone to Seven Sisters Cliffs as well as visiting the other towns in the area. In all that time, there'd never been a cross word spoken between us. Each day we were together ended with us sleeping in each other's arms. There wasn't any place in the world I'd rather be.

When I opened my eyes, light was streaming in the window and I was in bed alone. I could hear Saint's voice from the other room. It sounded as though he was arguing with someone. I waited to make sure he was on the phone and there wasn't another person with him, before getting out of bed, putting on the shirt he'd worn the day before, and joining him in the kitchen.

"Good morning," I said when I saw his cell on the counter, the screen dark.

Saint pulled me into an embrace without responding.

"Difficult call?" I asked.

"My uncle got wind it was me buying the cottage. That's the delay."

"Why would he delay? I'd think he'd be happy to have it stay in the family."

He pulled a chair away from the table, sat, and settled me on his lap. "In an interesting turn of events, he's anxious for me to return to London."

"Did he say why?"

"Evidently, there's something besides the cottage he wants to discuss with me. I'm guessing it's a matter he'd like me to look into on his behalf. In an official capacity, that is."

"Does that mean you'd get your job back?"

Saint shook his head. "This is merely an assignment to see if I'm worthy of an offer to return."

I was certainly no expert on MI6, but even I could see his uncle was manipulating him. "I don't like the sound of this."

"Neither do I."

"I don't know much about anything, but it seems like he's using you."

"You know everything." Saint grasped the back of my neck and kissed me. He angled his head to go deeper and sneaked his hand between my legs. He groaned, perhaps at my lack of panties or maybe because I was already so wet for him.

He drew back and looked into my eyes. "I want you endlessly."

"I feel the same." I leaned down and kissed the side of his neck.

"However, there are things we need to talk about." He shifted, moving me off his lap, stood, then motioned for me to sit in the chair we'd just vacated. He walked over to the kitchen counter and returned with two cups of coffee.

Since we arrived at the cottage, he hadn't made tea in the morning, only coffee. When I asked about it, he said he preferred it but Miss Bardwell still insisted on tea, no matter how often he asked otherwise.

I took a sip. "What things?"

"He's also insisting we join him and my aunt for dinner."

"I'm sure it will be fine, Saint."

"Tonight."

"Does he always request a command performance?"

Saint scooted his chair closer to me and moved mine so my legs were between his. He put his hands on my hips. "He does not."

"How did you respond?"

"I tried declining, but he was quite insistent."

"If you want to go on your own…" What? Could I offer to stay here? Or return to London and stay at his flat?

"Harper?"

I looked into his mesmerizing blue eyes.

"Where I go, you go too. Or vice versa. Even when you're in seminary class, or whatever you call it, I'll be sitting outside the door, waiting to walk you to your next."

I laughed and was about to suggest we go back to bed when his cell phone rang again.

"It's the man who found your ex and got your money back." He accepted the call and when I stood, tried to pull me back into the chair.

"Bathroom," I whispered, and he let go.

20

Saint

"I'm just about to board a plane headed your way," said Decker Ashford when I answered his call.

"You are? What's bringing you to London?"

"Quick stopover for Mila, Huck, and me on our way to Mallorca."

"Mallorca?" Why in the devil would Decker be taking his wife and baby son there?

"For Rile's wedding. That reminds me, he said you didn't RSVP."

"I didn't get an invitation." The familiar feeling of being excluded sat heavy on my chest.

"The hell you didn't. I vetted everyone on the list, and that included you."

I ran my hand through my hair. Had I truly been invited? "When is it?"

"Next weekend. You gonna make it?"

"Is it too late to vet a plus one?"

Decker laughed. "You don't seriously think she hasn't been already?"

There was no reason for either of us to qualify who we were talking about. "I'll message him now and offer my apologies for my late response."

"Good deal."

"Where are you staying in London?"

"Not far from you. The Wellesley."

Harper came out of the lavatory but went straight into the bedroom.

"I know you're on holiday, but I'm wondering if you'd have time for a brief meeting?" I asked.

"I was about to ask you the same thing, Saint. Gotta run now, though. I'll be in touch after we're settled."

I walked into the bedroom in search of Harper and found her packing. "I've been meaning to talk to you about that." I waved my hand at her luggage. "Perhaps it's time you had a place to put your things."

She flushed. Red, not pink.

I walked over and put my hands on her shoulders. "What's wrong?"

"I feel like a gypsy." She plopped down on the bed with a heavy sigh. "I don't know. Maybe this is crazy."

Every muscle in my body tensed. "What's crazy?"

"Alfriston. Being a vicar's assistant. What am I even doing?"

The tautness eased a bit at not hearing my name mentioned in the list. "What would you do if you returned to the States?"

She shrugged. "I guess I'd either continue on at Belmont or look for somewhere to complete my advanced degree."

"You said you weren't certain about your field, and yet here, you seemed excited."

When Harper rested her head on my shoulder, my muscles turned to mush in relief. I wasn't the specific cause of her uncertainty; the ease with which things fell together for her was.

"You told me you believe we were meant to meet."

"I do."

"I believe it too. What's more, I believe in you, Harper."

"Why?"

I shifted my body and hers so we were lying on the bed, and pulled her into my arms. "The same reason you believe in me."

"But, I'm—"

"I'm a bloody wanker for always interrupting you, and I don't know what disparaging thing you meant to say about yourself, but I won't allow it. I've never met anyone like you, and I mean that in the absolute most positive way. You're smart and funny, the most down-to-earth, accepting, giving, warm, wonderful, beautiful, sexy person I've ever known."

She buried her face in my shoulder, but I heard her whisper, "Thanks."

"Have I told you that when we first met, you reminded me of someone?"

"No."

"I spoke of her, though. Dr. Charles. She's the woman at MIT I was assigned to recruit as an MI6 asset."

She raised her head. "I remind you of her? Boy, are you off base!"

"Given you know little about her, I wonder what makes you say that."

"Expert on foreign policy compared to church leadership. Slightly different."

"Until I met you, I believed Emerson Charles had the purest heart I'd ever known. She doesn't hold a candle to you."

"Were you in love with her?"

"I fancied myself to be. I was wrong, though."

"How do you know you were wrong?"

I put Harper's hand on my heart. "Because what I feel here when I'm with you is unlike anything I've ever known."

"Saint, I—"

"I realize I'm being a wanker yet again, interrupting you, but I must. This is going to come out wrong, but I hope you'll give me the benefit of the doubt, like you always do."

"Say it."

"It doesn't matter how you feel, Harper. What I feel for you isn't dependent upon that. You don't need to let me down easy by saying we hardly know each other or you simply don't share my over-the-top declaration of affection. Nothing you say will change what's in here." I squeezed her hand that still rested on my heart. "I have one more thing to say."

"Okay," she whispered.

"I've never felt the sense of peace I do when I'm with you. I was a man without a mission, as they say. Or in my case, without a job. I saw no way around that, other than by completely changing my personality. That alone was a setup for failure. How does one change their personality? Anyway, I don't feel that way anymore. What I know I need to do is find a place where I fit. In the same way you fit here, in Alfriston."

I waited for her to speak. Perhaps I'd stunned her with my proclamations. Or maybe she was afraid if she tried, I'd talk over her again.

"Harper, please tell me what you're thinking. I can't bear not knowing."

She sat partway up, leaned on her elbow, and took my hand. When she rested it on her left breast, absolute tosser that I am, I squeezed it; Harper laughed but held my hand there anyway.

"What I feel here when I'm with you is unlike any-thing I've known. I couldn't bear not knowing how you felt about me." The words she used were almost verbatim of things I'd said.

"What do we do now?"

She shrugged again. "I guess you could ask me to move in with you. If you want to, that is. I'm kind of out of my element here. Dave didn't even want to have sex with me."

I pulled her down so her head rested on my chest. "I have a request."

"What is it?"

"Never use those words—Dave and sex—together again. As for the other thing you said, about me asking you to move in with me, you should know that I had second thoughts about buying Fox Run until I knew you wanted to be in Alfriston. I already own a flat I'm never at. Since wherever you are is where I want to be, I wondered if I should hold off until you knew."

"What if I go back to America?"

"I will follow wherever you lead, Harper Godfrey. You are my touchstone."

"So, I guess I'm moving in."

"That, you are. I'm about to say another thing that will likely come out all wrong."

She put her arm around my waist and squeezed. "Go ahead."

"While I'd be more than happy if you remained *sans clothes* day and night—while we're at home and alone—I'm wondering if you're feeling as though you need more."

"If you mean clothes, then, yes. I didn't see much in the way of clothing stores around here, but I figured they must have loads in London."

"Which reminds me. Dinner. We should probably be on our way by early afternoon."

"Since you mentioned it, I'd like to buy something a little less drab to wear tonight."

Harper in sackcloth would still be lovely as far as I was concerned, but I'd gladly do her bidding. "I'm reminded of something else. Two things, actually."

"Yes?"

"It's been brought to my attention that I somehow missed the invitation and subsequent RSVP for a friend's wedding. I have since made amends, or intend to, and was wondering if you'd join me. It's to be held on the island of Mallorca."

"Wow."

"And it's next weekend."

"Was there anything else?"

"I'm sorry?"

"You said you were reminded of two things."

"Before I answer, does 'wow' mean you're agreeing to join me?"

"I suppose I must if wherever you go, I follow." She winked at me.

"Quite the opposite, my darling."

Her cheeks pinkened, and she cast her gaze downward.

"Tell me what you're thinking."

"I like it when you call me your darling."

"Then, I shall do it every day."

"How soon do we have to leave?"

I checked the time. "Not for another hour or so."

When Harper unfastened the buttons on the shirt she was wearing and let it fall to the floor, all thoughts of what I wanted to tell her about my uncle vanished.

21

Harper

My eyes almost popped out of my head when I saw the prices of the dresses in the boutique Saint brought me to. While I hadn't expected it would be on par with the discount and secondhand shops where I usually bought my clothes, I didn't expect a single dress to cost more than my first car. It wasn't even an evening gown. Just a dress.

"I've made a mess of this too, haven't I?" Saint asked, snaking his arm around my waist.

"It isn't you. I'm just not used to…"—I lowered my voice—"everything being so expensive."

"My apologies. I've just received a message from Eliza, who first berated me for bringing you here and, second, recommended another shop you might enjoy more."

"Thank you," I said to the woman who'd been staring at us with folded arms. She resembled the flight attendant Saint had said was wearing too much "batter."

Which reminded me. "I, um, don't usually wear much makeup, so I didn't bring any to London with me," I said once we were out of the boutique.

Saint stopped walking and cupped my cheek. "You don't need it. You're absolutely flawless without it."

"You're very sweet to me."

"And you're very beautiful. Oh, and Eliza sends her apologies that she won't be joining us tonight. Hot date she evidently didn't want to cancel."

"I'll be okay with your uncle, Saint. Neither you nor Eliza needs to be so worried." I stood on my tiptoes and kissed him.

"Oh, I like that very much," he murmured before angling his head to go deeper. When he ended our kiss and I opened my eyes, I saw someone duck around the corner. There was something odd about it.

"Everything okay?" he asked.

"Maybe your paparazzi."

"Where?"

I pointed behind us.

"Let's be on our way, then." Saint took my arm and led me over to his car.

"You're worried," I said when he got in the driver's side.

"Occupational hazard." He drove a short distance away and parked.

"It's so close; we could've walked."

"Ready?" he asked, motioning to the boutique adjacent to where we had stopped.

After the last store, I no longer felt like shopping, but I didn't want to embarrass Saint by showing up at his uncle's house looking like a ragamuffin, as my grandmother used to say. I just hoped there was something I could afford at this one. Maybe I'd find something I could wear both to dinner tonight and to the wedding next weekend.

After an hour, we left with two dresses, three pairs of pants, four sweaters, a jacket, and two pairs of boots. Saint convinced me I would soon need it all as the weather got colder both in London and in Alfriston.

I'd hoped to see Miss Bardwell when we arrived at the flat, but Saint said she usually didn't stay past noon when he wasn't there.

"What time is dinner?" I asked, realizing he'd never said.

He was studying something on his phone. "Eight."

"What time do we need to leave?"

"Sorry?"

"Saint, is everything okay?"

"Yes, fine." He set his phone down and looked at me for maybe the first time since we arrived at the flat. "My apologies, Harper. Habit, I suppose. Anyway, to answer your question honestly, no, everything is not okay." He walked over and poured himself a drink. "Fancy one?"

I shook my head. I took the glass from his hand and pulled him over to the sofa. "No, thanks. Why don't you talk to me instead? Tell me what's got you so rattled."

"I received a message from Adam Benjamin, saying he's on his way to Hong Kong."

"Oh." I understood why Saint was so out of sorts. He'd put the man off three times, and now he'd gone off on his own.

"You must be feeling like you let him down."

He rested his back on the sofa and looked up at the ceiling. "It's like watching the same train wreck about to happen twice. The last time he pulled this, I went after him and we both landed in a Chinese detention center."

"What will you do this time?"

He turned his head and looked into my eyes. "I honestly don't know. I suppose that's why I'm so bloody frustrated."

"What else is bothering you?"

"How do you know there's something else?"

"Your tension is palpable, Saint."

"I don't know whether to marvel at you or be terrified that you can read my mind."

"It isn't your mind. Your moods are very easy to read."

"I'm thirty years old, and I don't think anyone has said anything like that to me, ever."

"Maybe you never let anyone get close enough to."

"Or maybe I was just waiting for you."

"Stop trying to skirt the subject. What else is bothering you?"

"Compared to Adam, it's nothing."

I raised a brow and folded my arms.

Saint laughed. "That's the same look you had on your face on the plane when you were trying to get me to talk by keeping your mouth full of cheesecake."

"It worked."

"To a certain extent. What you didn't know was how much I wanted to lick away the bit of strawberry that lingered on your lips."

When I didn't respond, he sighed and picked up a framed photograph sitting on the table beside him. It was of a woman.

"Today was my mother's birthday."

"What happened to her, Saint?"

He stood to get another drink, and this time, I didn't try to stop him. "It isn't something I talk about." He kept his back to me long enough that I considered going into the bedroom I'd slept in when I first arrived to let him have some space.

"There was an accident," he said without turning around to face me. "My mother was thrown from a horse during a hunting event she hadn't wanted to attend but my father insisted."

"I'm so sorry."

"She lingered on the brink of death for several days before finally succumbing to her injuries." His voice sounded so different. Almost robotic.

He finished the liquor in his glass and faced me. "As you can imagine, my father was racked with guilt. I was attending university at the time and, in hindsight, shouldn't have returned after my mother's funeral."

"How old were you when it happened?"

"Nineteen when she died."

"And your father?"

"I had just turned twenty when I got the call that he'd been in an automobile accident. The autopsy indicated he had three times the legal limit of alcohol in his bloodstream when he crashed his car into a tree."

I wanted to comfort him, but he was the one who'd put the space between us, and I respected his need. "I'll let you have some time on your own if you'd like."

He crossed the room in what felt like a split second, sat beside me on the sofa, took off my glasses, and put his arm around my shoulders. "God, I'm sorry. You don't need to hear all this."

It felt so good to have him close, I rested my head on his chest and put my arm around his waist. "I asked, Saint."

"That didn't give me the right to dump it all on you. Look, I'll call and tell them we have to cancel tonight. I don't want to subject you to even more."

"No. Let's go." I didn't want to say so we could just get it over with, but that's how I felt.

"If you're certain you want to go through with it, I suppose we could manage a quick dinner and be on our way."

Something in my gut told me it couldn't possibly be that easy.

22

Saint

The moment we walked in, I knew this was a bad idea. My uncle was up to something; I was certain of it.

"Welcome, Niven," said Aunt Millicent. She approached, cheek-kissed me, and proceeded to look Harper up and down as if she was summing her up.

"Niven," said my uncle.

"Nigel, you remember Harper Godfrey. Harper, this is my aunt, Millicent."

"It's a pleasure to meet you," Harper said graciously but without her usual step forward to shake hands. "Hello, sir," she said to Nigel.

"Come in, come in." My uncle motioned to the drawing room. "Can I get you a drink?"

"Water, please," answered Harper. Nigel raised a brow and looked at me.

"I'll have the same, thank you."

I saw a look pass between him and my aunt.

"Very well," he said, pouring himself a scotch and making no move to bring us our requested water. "I asked you here tonight to discuss Fox Run Cottage. I have a proposal for you."

Here it came, whatever it was he wanted me to do for him in order to secure my former position at MI6. I was glad he'd brought this up before we sat down to eat, given the subject made my stomach turn.

"Uncle, I must insist you not do this. I will not take on an assignment on your behalf just to secure a job."

"An assignment? I've no idea what you're talking about. My proposal relates to your marriage."

"Your what?" gasped Harper. Looking at her ashen face, I realized my mistake in bringing her here. When we ran into my uncle at Buckingham Palace, I'd worried he would think I'd heeded his advice and might say something that would make Harper think I was using her. How could I have not forewarned her about this?

She leaned closer to me and whispered, "You're married?"

"No, he's not," my uncle answered before I could. "And that's what I'd like to discuss. I'm curious as to why you haven't yet announced an engagement. My sources tell me you and Miss Godfrey have been living together at the cottage. This is not the arrangement we discussed, Niven."

Harper studied me. "Arrangement?"

"There is no arrangement," I assured her. "Uncle, my being with Harper has nothing whatsoever to do with your demands that I marry."

He shook his head and smirked. "So, you haven't confided in her yet. Well, the cat is out of the bag now, as they say."

"No. It's nothing like that." I turned to Harper. "I need you to believe me. I have no arrangement and have nothing to confide in you."

Her eyes stayed fixed on mine, but I couldn't read her thoughts. Was she doubting me?

She turned and looked first at my aunt, then at Nigel. "You said you have a proposal regarding Fox Run Cottage. What is it?"

"Any proposals are off the table," I spat, ready to stand and tell Harper it was time for us to leave.

"No, I'd like to hear what he has to say."

My uncle got an evil glint in his eye. "Not quite as innocent as I thought. I suppose the fact that you've been sleeping with him should've made me realize that sooner."

"That's it. We're going." I stood and held my hand out to Harper.

She shook her head. "We're not leaving until we hear your uncle out."

As much as I didn't want to, I sat back down. "Very well, get on with it."

"I will grant you both unlimited access to Fox Run Cottage once you've announced your engagement, during which time I will make arrangements for a prenuptial agreement to be drawn up."

"You bloody wanker," I muttered under my breath.

"Once you're married, I will allow you to purchase it as a wedding gift. After your eventual divorce, Niven will retain sole ownership of the estate as per the prenup."

I sat in stunned silence. He considered allowing me to buy the cottage a gift?

"How long do you see this marriage lasting?" Harper asked before I could get my wits about me.

"No more than five years."

"What about children?"

"There will be none as per the agreement you will sign before the wedding."

I stood again. "This conversation is over," I bellowed. "Harper, we're leaving. I'll listen to no more of this."

Thankfully, she stood too.

"I'll wait to hear your decision," I heard my uncle say as we left the room and walked into the foyer. "My offer is good for forty-eight hours. If I don't have your decision by then, you will forfeit any claim on Fox Run, and I will proceed with the sale to someone else."

I knew the last thing he said was bait, but the way I felt now, I didn't care if he had another buyer or not. I wanted nothing to do with the cottage or with him.

Once we were in the car, I turned to her. "Harper, I want you to know—"

"Saint, please, let's wait to discuss this at the flat."

"Of course." I was dizzy with the idea that this was the end for Harper and me. If I'd only confided in her about my uncle's demands before we went to their flat, this all could have been avoided. Now it was too late.

"You said there were other things we needed to talk about," Harper said once we arrived and she'd taken a seat in the living room. "Was this it?"

"It was." I walked over and poured myself a drink. There was no way I could get through this conversation without one.

"I'd like one, please," Harper said just as I was getting ready to take a seat.

"Certainly." I handed her my glass, poured another, and sat beside her.

"Was this what you meant when you said your uncle wanted you to change your personality?"

"I suppose so, yes." While I was prone to interrupting Harper more often than not, something told me to hear her out. "My uncle has insisted I marry."

"Has he chosen your future wife? Is that why your ex is coming back to London?"

"Not at all." Was it? No, Nigel wouldn't have proposed the arrangement for me to take ownership of Fox Run if that was the plan. Although, there was the possibility he'd announced his idea in front of Harper rather than with me alone with the hope she would end things with me and return to America.

"Saint?"

"You asked if Nigel had chosen my future wife. I don't believe so. He did suggest a certain type, though."

"I see." Harper frowned and gulped her drink.

"I don't think you do."

"Saint, please. Just get to the point." I hated the annoyance in her voice, especially given I knew this was the end for us.

I took a deep breath and let it out slowly. "His exact words were, 'Not one of those trollops you so often parade about with. Find yourself a nice young lady.' The day he showed up at Buckingham Palace and gave you the third degree, I feared he thought I heeded his advice."

She took off her glasses and rubbed her eyes. This was it, I could feel her rejection coming, and I had no idea what to do to change her mind.

"Harper?"

"Yes?"

"You know that isn't the case, right?"

"I'm not a nice young lady?"

"You are the nicest young lady I've known in my life. What I meant was, I didn't seek you out because of it." I could swear I saw the hint of her dimples.

"You mean you didn't know a woman who had just been jilted at the altar *and* wanted to be a minister had an open seat next to her on that plane?" She smiled, and so did I.

"Do I dare hope you're not breaking things off with me, then?"

"Why would I do that?"

"If you thought I was using you."

She leaned closer, and I put my arm around her shoulders. When I did, she rested her head on my chest. "I would never think that."

"Thank God."

She leaned up and kissed my cheek. "I know you better than that, Saint."

I rubbed my chest where her head had been. The relief I felt was palpable. That Harper believed me, more, had never doubted me, almost brought me to tears. This woman was truly a gift from God. "You soothe me, Harper. Way down deep in my soul. Your unwavering belief in me is humbling."

I didn't disturb Harper's sleep the next morning when I woke. It had been an emotional night followed by my endless need to have my mouth, hands, or cock ravishing some part of her body.

As I drank the tea Miss Bardwell made for me, I thought about how soon we'd be able to return to Alfriston—a place that remained special to me regardless of my uncle's attempt to tarnish it. I wondered if Harper would want to visit London Seminary either today or tomorrow. From there, I hoped she chose to apply either to it or the University of Sussex rather than return to school in the US.

Left unsettled was the status of Fox Run. My uncle rightfully owned it. While last night I'd questioned whether I even wanted to buy it, by light of day, it meant far more to me than just having been in our family for four hundred years. It was the place where Harper and I had first made love. More, the first time she'd ever made love. To me, it made Fox Run sacred.

If my uncle still intended to sell, I didn't see a legal way for him to prevent me from making an offer. If mine wasn't the highest, I could increase it.

While that was all well and good, if he retained ownership, it left the question of where Harper and I would stay when in Alfriston, which we would have to do if she was to be of any assistance to the vicar. It would be impossible to commute back and forth from London, given it was two hours each way.

If anyone would know of something available for rent, I was sure it would be Barbara, the neighbor and property agent who was handling the sale of the cottage.

I called and left a message, letting her know I was in the market for a rental property for now, and perhaps something to purchase in the future.

She called back a few minutes later. "Does this mean you're no longer interested in the cottage?"

"I wasn't certain if my uncle took it off the market."

"I've heard nothing about that. The last I knew, he wanted to further negotiate directly with you."

As he had done and failed. "I have reason to believe he may change his mind about selling."

"I suppose now is as good a time as any for me to bring something to your attention. I hope I'm not over-stepping by doing so."

"Go ahead."

"I was reviewing the title history, and there is a stipulation that a sale cannot take place without prior approval from all other heirs. That would include a sale to you."

"Meaning what exactly?"

"Obtaining approval would be part of the escrow process. What I'm uncertain of is if he can even *sell* it to you or any other heir."

"Are you saying he would have to *give* it to another heir?"

"That's my understanding, but you might want to have a solicitor look into it."

"Thank you for this information."

I rang off, stunned by what she'd just. There were two heirs other than my uncle—Eliza and me. As I'd already discussed the matter with her, I knew she didn't want the cottage. However, if what Barbara said was correct, that it would have to be deeded rather than sold to an heir might make her change her mind.

I sent two text messages. The first asking my cousin to contact me at her earliest convenience. The second was to Decker Ashford, hoping we could meet today. If so, I'd be adding another item to the agenda. If anyone could find out the exact stipulations of a possible sale, it would be him.

23

Harper

"I blame myself," said Eliza shortly after she'd arrived at the flat and Saint excused himself to take a call.

"Why?"

"I know my father. If I'd been there last night, he wouldn't have pulled the stunt he did."

"Whether he would have last night or not doesn't matter. He would have eventually."

"If I hadn't been so caught up in a *muy caliente* Spaniard, I may have been able to talk some sense into Father." She put her hand on my shoulder and looked into my eyes. "You're so good for my cousin. I hate to think anything my father said would change your opinion of him."

"Never."

"My dad has always tried to control Niven, but you know as well as I do, there isn't a man less likely to allow it." She studied me. "He's the most independent person I've known in my life, and yet, I sense his soul would be lost without you."

"I don't know about that."

"Well, I do. I can tell by the way he looks at you."

"It's me who would be lost without him."

"You needn't worry about Niven. He's invincible."

I raised a brow.

"What?" she asked.

"He'd like to be."

"Now I'm confused."

"What made you use that word?"

Eliza shrugged. "I don't know. I guess it's just the way I've always seen him."

I knew better than to mention that the word she'd used was the name of the firm he hoped to work for. Instead, I changed the subject. "Tell me more about the Spaniard."

Eliza's cheeks flushed like mine so often did. "He's a god."

"I want to hear all about him." I half listened as she extolled the virtues of a man she'd known a week, and then I realized how judgmental I sounded, given Saint and I hadn't been together that long.

When Saint came out of the bedroom at the very end of the hallway, he appeared distracted.

"Eliza. You're still here."

She looked at me, and I shrugged.

"Niven, you invited me."

"Right, right. Sorry."

"Shall I come back some other time?"

"No. Now's good."

Saint ran his hand through his hair, and his eyes met mine.

"I'll just excuse myself."

"No, I'd rather you hear this too. Especially after last night."

24

Saint

I'd just finished telling Eliza and Harper what I learned from the property manager when I received a text from Decker, saying he'd arrived.

Not wanting to know whether he could hack into the building's security, I offered to meet him in the lobby.

"Thanks for agreeing to this," I said, escorting him into the lift.

"It's as much for me as it is you."

"If there's time, I have another situation I want to run past you."

He nodded and walked out when the doors opened into my foyer. "Harper Godfrey, I presume. I'm Decker Ashford."

Harper stood and walked over to him, stunning me when she embraced him. "Thank you for helping me."

"It's what we do." Our eyes met, and I realized I hadn't properly thanked him for getting Harper's money back.

"My appreciation as well, Decker."

"Niven, if we're finished with our discussion, I'll say my goodbyes." Eliza gathered her purse and sweater.

"We are, for now. By the way, Decker, this is my cousin, Eliza. Eliza, meet Decker Ashford."

"I'll say hello and farewell at the same time," she said, shaking his hand.

Decker nodded but didn't say anything in response, which wasn't like him.

"So, Harper, will we be seeing you at the wedding?"

She looked at me, and I nodded.

"We've officially sent our response and are looking forward to it."

"Glad to hear it. We'll have more time to socialize then."

Bright woman that she was, Harper picked up on Decker's hint that we needed to get on with our meeting.

"If you'll excuse me," she said, heading down the hallway to the bedroom.

"She's somethin'," Decker said after Harper closed the door behind her.

"She's everything."

Decker smiled. "I know the feeling."

"How is Mila? She and the baby are here with you, are they not?"

"They are, which means I need to make this quick."

"My office is this way, if you'd like to meet there," I motioned in the direction Harper had gone.

"I think it's best, given what we need to discuss."

"Would you like to go first, or shall I?" I asked once we were seated with the door closed.

"I will. It's come to my attention that Dr. Benjamin has pulled a disappearing-into-Hong-Kong act for the second time. When he did this before, it was our crew who went in and pulled both him and you out."

I opened my mouth to speak, but Decker held up his hand.

"You did the exact right thing on that mission, Saint. I don't care what MI6 or anyone else says. If you hadn't gone in after him, you would have been abandoning your assigned mission. Don't think others haven't taken notice of that. In my opinion, it was MI6 who was wrong, and I didn't hesitate to let Z know that."

Z Alexander, the current chief of Military Intelligence Section 6, was also Decker Ashford's adopted father.

"I appreciate you offering your opinion on my behalf."

"That brings us to Lynx Edgemon."

I took a deep breath and let it out slowly. Lynx had been my handler when I went in after Benjamin the last time. While it was Z's decision to sack me, I was disappointed when Lynx didn't put up more of an argument. Lynx was a partner in Decker's firm now, and thus, I'm sure he had a say in whom they made offers of employment to. Not that I knew that was what Decker was here to discuss. Suspecting it was, I anticipated the need for an apology.

"I understand. Say no more."

He laughed. "You're gonna want to let me finish."

I shook my head. "Sorry, Deck."

"As I was saying, Lynx came to us after the extraction and the subsequent interrogation on the Operation Whistleblower mission. He suggested bringing you on board as a permanent part of the team."

I was stunned and said so.

"The rest of the partners had to vote, but we all knew it would be unanimous." He handed me an envelope. "This is your partnership offer."

"Did you say *partnership*?" I'd expected to be offered a role in an upcoming mission, but as a contractor, not an employee. I never would've considered a buy-in as a remote possibility.

"I did, and I'll leave this with you. Take a look at our offer and run it by your attorney. Hell, you could even have Z take a look at it on your behalf. Although if you do that, he'll probably up the offer I know MI6 is about to extend. So maybe don't go to him for advice." Decker winked. "The bottom line is we want you on our team, Saint. We'd be proud to have you join us."

"I don't know what to say. I truly did not see this coming."

"Yeah, you're all humble and shit. You're gonna have to let that go if you're plannin' on bein' an Invincible." Decker shook his head. "I always hated that name. Fuckin' Rile."

It was widely known that Rile DeLéon had come up with the Invincible Intelligence and Security Group moniker and was intransigent about calling it anything else. Given he'd been the one to approach the other founding partners about starting the firm, he saw it as his decision.

"Our next agenda item is Dr. Benjamin. We're prepared to go in and get him whether you sign on the bottom line or not. We owe him that much after the help he gave us with the whistleblower. Now, if it were up to me, I would've made you sign on the dotted line first."

"Listen, Deck, to be honest with you, I've wanted to be part of the Invincibles team since I first heard you gentlemen were in business." I held up the envelope. "I don't need to read this to give you my answer. I want in."

Decker reached out, and we shook hands. "Damn glad to hear it, and welcome. When you *do* get around to lookin' at the contract you're gonna need to sign, you'll see your compensation package is generous. Okay, now that that's out of the way, let's talk about Benjamin."

What I learned was that the doctor had seemingly disappeared into thin air. There was no intel on his whereabouts, and even Decker's facial recognition technologies hadn't turned up anything.

That could very well mean Benjamin had been taken in by Chinese authorities like he and I both had been hours after arriving in Hong Kong the last time we were there. But if that were the case, we would've heard he'd been detained. The US and UK spy networks in both Hong Kong and on the mainland were vast.

"I'm not sure you'll be able to find out any more about his whereabouts than I have, but let me know if you do. In the meantime, we need to assemble the extraction team. And by we, I mean you, Saint."

I had no idea where to begin. While I knew all the partners and some of the contractors, I had no way of knowing who might be available.

"Where's your laptop?" Deck asked.

"Here." I stood and took it out of my desk drawer.

"Your security clearances and access to the Invincibles website was set up before the last mission. If you let me borrow that for a minute, I'll set up your access to the rest. Mainly, the list of who is available and their twenty."

"Appreciate it."

"I see deployment happening almost immediately after getting a read on where he is. There's one guy I'd like to recommend to you as a second, Rip Kailor."

"I've worked with Rip."

"He's a good man, excellent with technology. I'm groomin' him to take on more of what I do now that Huck's arrived. I want to spend more time bein' a dad."

"Understood. Shall I make contact?"

"Your mission, Saint. Do as you see fit."

"Roger that. If there's nothing else on Dr. Benjamin at this time, there's something else I'd like to talk to you about."

"As you said."

After I explained what I'd learned from Barbara about Fox Run Cottage, Decker promised to look into it.

"See you Saturday, if not before."

"Looking forward to it."

"It'll be the perfect time to introduce you as the newest partner, so sign the damned contract."

"I will do, and thank you again, Decker."

I walked him out and was about to go into the bedroom in search of Harper when I realized I had a dilemma, one I hadn't been faced with at any other time in my career. I couldn't confide any of the impending mission's details in Harper, both for her safety and mine. Benjamin's too, really. Since I'd never had cause to share details with anyone outside of an assignment before, I had no idea how to handle it.

Everything I'd told her about when the doctor and I had been detained and then extracted, had been post-op. I may have overshared some of the details, but nothing that would've put anyone in danger.

"Is everything okay?" she asked when I opened the bedroom door and found her reading in a chair by the window.

"I'm a bit out of my element."

She set her book down and leaned forward. "What do you mean?"

"I'm not at liberty to share with you some of the things discussed in our meeting."

"It makes sense there would be."

"But I've never struggled with it before. It's been a nonissue."

Harper smiled, catching me off guard.

"What?"

"It's okay that you can't tell me."

"I admit I am often daft, but why does it make you happy?"

"Because you want to."

I smiled too. "This will not be easy for me to navigate. I may muck it up from time to time, but never because of you."

"If I become a minister, there will be things I can't tell you, either."

"I hadn't thought of that." I rubbed my chin. "Like what?"

"If someone in the congregation confides in me, I will not be able to discuss whatever it is."

"On the plus side, you understand my dilemma."

"Of course I do."

"Would you like to hear the parts of my conversation with Decker I am able to share?"

"If you want to tell me."

"Did you want to tell me about your initial conversation with Reverend Primrose when he offered you the position of curate?"

"I couldn't wait."

"A sentiment I'm familiar with."

She smiled again, exposing her lovely dimples. "Hurry and tell me."

"I've been offered a partnership."

She cocked her head. "Is that what you wanted?"

"Several steps above what I wanted."

She jumped up, clapping her hands before throwing her arms around my neck. "I'm so happy for you, Saint. And it's all on your own merit, not because you made a deal with someone in order for them to help you."

I hadn't thought of it that way, but I hoped she was right and there were no caveats in their offer.

25

Harper

As we drove up to Heathrow Airport, a torrent of feelings I hadn't anticipated swept over me.

"How are you feeling about flying today?" Saint asked on our drive from his flat to the airport the day before the wedding.

"Not bad. As long as you let me hold your hand during takeoff."

"You had quite the death grip on the armrest."

"I promise not to break the bones in your fingers."

"Then, we have a deal."

The last time I was here, I'd felt so lost and alone, and then it got worse. I thanked God for bringing Saint into my life every time I prayed, but thinking back on all he'd done for me, when he could easily have left me to fend for myself, made me appreciate him all the more.

Being here also reminded me how long it had been since I talked to either of my parents or Mouse. I needed to call her and my mother, at least. I still wasn't speaking to my dad. I doubted he'd ever admit, or even realize, the bind he'd put me in when he refused to give me the money for a ticket.

I looked over at Saint, who squeezed my hand.

"I'm so very happy you're with me, Harper."

"I feel the same."

"There's something else on your mind, isn't there?"

I sighed. "My dad. I'm still mad at him, but do you realize that if he had given me the money to get home, I wouldn't be here with you? It made me think that maybe I should thank him."

He brought my hand to his lips and kissed the back of it before turning it over and doing the same to my palm, only this time, he used his tongue. "I'm the one who should be giving him my thanks." When he leaned over and kissed me, I shuddered.

It had only been a couple of hours since Saint and I had made love, first in bed, then in the shower, and then back in bed again, but I already wanted more.

He reached under my sweater, moved the cup of my bra out of his way, and teased my nipple. I groaned.

"Not much longer until I can bury myself deep inside you," he whispered.

I looked up and into the rearview mirror to see if the driver, who I now knew as Miss Bardwell's brother, was paying any attention to us. Either he was oblivious or very good at pretending he was.

"How long is the flight?"

"Not long enough."

I cocked my head. First, he said it wouldn't be much longer until he could be inside me again, then he said the flight wouldn't be long enough. He wasn't making sense.

He pulled his hand from under my sweater and adjusted his pants. "You'll see, my darling."

Rather than stop where I saw departure signs, Mr. Bardwell kept going until we came to a fenced-off area and a guardhouse. Saint rolled down the window, and the man waved us in.

"Where are we going?"

He brought my hand to his mouth like he had earlier, except this time, he kissed my fingertips. He pointed outside the window on my side of the car. "There."

I saw a much smaller plane than any I'd been on before. "Is that yours?"

He smiled and shook his head. "It's a perk of being the newest partner in the Invincibles. They sent it so we didn't have to fly commercial."

If I thought flying first class was nice, once we were inside the corporate aircraft, the previous one reminded me of a bus. "It's gorgeous," I said, running my hand over the supple leather seats that looked more like regular chairs. There were even a couple of sofas.

"Come with me, and I'll show you the best part." He led me to the back of the plane and opened a door. "Go ahead."

I gasped when I stepped inside and saw a king-size bed. "Wow."

"Wow is right. This is where you and I will be shortly after takeoff."

"Seriously?"

"Would that we could occupy it now, but we cannot."

"How long did you say the flight was?"

"Less than three hours."

That was plenty of time to pick up where we'd left off this morning, and on a plane no less. I felt my face flush and lowered my gaze. "I think we'll be able to make good use of the time, don't you?"

Saint groaned. "You little minx."

As soon as the pilot signaled we could leave our seats, Saint and I hurried to the stateroom.

"You know what to do, my darling."

I already had most of my clothes off and was waiting for his next instructions.

"On the bed, legs spread."

I did as he told me and waited for Saint to remove his clothes. Instead, he knelt between my legs, put his hands on my knees, and spread me open more.

Slowly torturing me, he kissed and licked his way up my body. When he reached the top of my thigh, he blew on my pussy in that way he knew sent shivers up my spine and had me writhing in anticipation of what he'd do with his mouth.

"You're very wet for me, Harper."

"I always am, Saint."

"Do you know what I'm going to do to you?"

I nodded.

"Use your words, my darling."

"You're going to make me come so hard that stars will swirl around me."

"Mmm. I like it when you talk dirty." He thrust a finger inside me and lashed my clit with his tongue. "Let me feel you. Squeeze my finger." He added a second digit and licked from where his fingers were up to my clit. When he fastened his mouth to it, I took off like a rocket.

Saint continued toying with me while I rode the climax out, then moved up my body to kiss me. When I reached for him, he grabbed my wrist. "What's wrong?"

"Nothing. As long as I'm with you, nothing is ever wrong."

"Then, why don't you want me to touch you?"

"I want to talk to you instead."

I smiled. "You're weird, but okay, if you want to give me mindless pleasure and then have a conversation instead of letting me have my wicked way with you, that's your choice."

He laughed and turned so he was on his side. "You're absolutely adorable and a terrible tease, but what I have to say is important."

I sat up. "Should I get dressed?"

"No. I want to be able to look at what's mine."

I brought my legs together, but Saint pushed them apart. "Mine. Do you understand what I'm saying, Harper? You're mine. All mine. No one else will ever see your beautiful pussy or push their tongue into your mouth, sharing your taste with you. No one will bury their face between your breasts, and no one will ever know what it feels like to have their cock buried so deep inside you, their balls ache."

I knew better than to move, but when Saint ran his fingertips up and down my leg, I grabbed his hand and put it on my pussy.

"Yes, my darling. This is mine." He took my hand and put it on his cock. "And this is yours. All yours. No one else will wrap their hand around me or swirl their tongue around its tip. No one will suck me in so deep that I forget my own name. No one."

I was so turned on—again—I couldn't stop my body from writhing. "I need you inside me, Saint. Please."

"Soon. I promise."

Unless it was in the next second, it wouldn't be soon enough for me. I was about to do something I'd never done and start tearing Saint's clothes from his body the way he sometimes tore mine.

"First, close your eyes."

I did so gladly. Saint always did wondrous things to me when he demanded I keep them shut. Instead of his mouth on or fingers in my pussy, I felt Saint's hand wrapped around my left wrist. He slid something cold on the third finger of my left hand.

"Open, Harper."

I raised my hand and looked at the most beautiful ring I'd ever seen. There was an emerald-cut diamond in the center, flanked by tapered baguette-cut diamonds.

"Marry me, Harper."

I looked from the ring into his eyes, never more certain that this was the absolute right thing. Saint and I were meant to be together. Whether fate or God had intervened, I believed that with all my heart.

"I know what you're going to say." He smiled, his beautiful eyes sparkling.

"You do?"

"You're going to say yes. I know it. Do you want to know how I know?"

I smiled and leaned forward, and he kissed my left dimple. "Sure."

"You never would have given yourself to me if you didn't believe one day we'd be man and wife."

It was true. The first time Saint and I made love, I had no question about whether it was right. I knew, like he said, that one day, he'd be my husband. I trusted him unequivocally.

"Yes, I'll marry you, Saint."

He kissed me hard, refusing to let his lips leave mine as we both struggled to get him out of his clothes.

When he was naked, he knelt between my legs. "I don't want anything between us, Harper."

"I could get pregnant."

"It would make me the happiest man alive."

I reached for him and guided him to my entrance. "Please, Saint. I need you inside me."

"Before I am, there's something else I need to say."

I smiled, beating him to the words I knew were coming. "I love you."

"I love you too, you little minx."

We spent the rest of the flight in each other's arms, making love again and again, even during the landing. After which, Saint thanked me for keeping him distracted.

When we got off the plane, a car was waiting near the bottom of the stairs. A man got out, but Saint opened the door for me instead. A bottle of champagne was on a table along with two glasses. He popped the cork, poured, and held up his glass after handing me mine.

"To the future Mrs. St. Thomas, the woman who made growing up worthwhile."

"Where are we?" I asked as we pulled up to a gate that looked like it led into a forest. "I say that a lot, don't I?" I giggled, and Saint kissed the tip of my nose, smiling. "The champagne is making me giggly."

"This is Rile's estate. I suppose I should've informed you of this sooner. Rile is the nephew of the King of Spain."

I gasped. "Will he be at the wedding?"

"I would be very surprised if he and the Queen were not."

"Wow."

"And speaking of queens, Rile is also related to another monarch."

"Are you saying what I think you're saying?"

"He is second cousin to the Queen of England."

"Now you're just being silly."

When Saint shrugged, I had a feeling he wasn't being silly at all.

Once beyond the gate, the drive took us through a forest of oak trees, past a grove of olive trees, and past two houses. I'd been wondering why the driver didn't stop when the view opened to the sea. I gasped.

"That is the Bay of Palma," said Saint, pointing. "And that is Rile's house."

I now understood why the driver hadn't stopped at the other two houses. "We aren't staying there, are we?"

"No, my darling. We'll be staying in town. There's a gathering here tonight, though. I can't wait for you to meet everyone."

26

Saint

For the first time in as long as I could remember—when Harper and I joined those gathered in the outside pavilion that overlooked the ocean—I felt as though I belonged. As I scanned the crowd, many made eye contact and waved. Decker abruptly left the conversation he was in the midst of and walked in our direction, his wife holding their son, beside him.

"Harper, Saint, welcome. This is my wife, Mila. Mila, meet Harper Godfrey. And this big fella is Huck."

The baby crawled into Deck's arms and buried his face in his father's shoulder. "He's gettin' tired," Decker explained, stroking the baby's cheek.

I thought about what Harper had said on the plane, that if we made love without protection, she might get pregnant. I'd told her it would make me the happiest man alive, and I meant it. Seeing Decker with his son not only warmed my heart, I was envious.

"Oh my God," I heard Mila gasp. "Decker, look!"

They eyed Harper's ring. "I knew it! I told Mila the next wedding we'd be celebrating was yours."

"Let's, please, keep this under wraps, as they say. This is Rile and Kensington's wedding celebration."

"I hear ya, Saint, but maybe you should've gotten Harper a ring that didn't blind everyone who looked at it." He lowered his voice. "I don't even wanna know how many carats that thing is."

What I didn't tell Decker—because I hadn't yet told Harper—was that the ring she wore, the ring she'd accepted as a promise to spend her life with me, had belonged to my mother. That was its worth. No amount of money could equal what my mother meant to me.

"Hey, uh, I don't want to spoil the excitement of your engagement or the wedding, but I did some digging into the thing you asked about the cottage."

"I'm assuming it isn't good news."

Decker rubbed his chin. "Depends on how you look at it."

"Is your intention to tease me all night, or are you going to get on with it?"

"Hey, sweetheart, would you mind taking over for a minute? Saint and I have something we need to discuss."

Mila held out her hands to the baby, but instead of reaching for his mother, he reached for Harper.

"A man after my own heart," I said, winking at her.

"Do you mind if I hold him?" Harper asked Mila.

"Not even a little. We might want to sit down, though; he gets heavy quick."

Decker and I watched the two women walk over to a table. "Shall we do this here or elsewhere?" I asked.

"Come with me."

I followed Decker down the trail to the beach. "Mila wasn't kidding about Huck getting heavy. Holding him wears me out." When we came to a bench, he sat. "Anyway, I didn't find anything on the title, but that doesn't mean I won't. It's a four-hundred-year-old house. God knows what the laws governing real estate were then."

"What *did* you find?"

"It's about your uncle, and it isn't good, Saint."

"Tell me."

"He's gotten himself deep in debt."

"How?"

"Not that I could see his bank records or anything…"

"Right," I muttered, knowing full well he could.

"It appears he's been living beyond his means for a number of years, although there have been significant increases in his spending in the last two."

"He's been jockeying for the foreign secretary position."

"I don't know much about UK politics, but I can tell you that the folks in political positions in the US certainly don't make their living from their salary."

"Right."

"Sorry, Saint."

"Not planning to shoot the messenger, Decker." I sat on the bench and looked up at the sky. "Bloody hell. When did the extravagant spending begin?"

"Goin' back at least thirty years. Eleven years, though, is when the amount of money coming in showed a big decrease."

That was when my mother died. I vaguely remembered arguments between her and my father about Nigel and Millicent. Could it have been over money? It wouldn't be difficult for someone like Decker to find out if she'd been supporting him.

"I have one more thing I'd like to ask you look into, if it isn't too much trouble."

Decker stood and patted my shoulder. "Already done, Saint, and the answer is yes."

"My mother?"

He nodded and walked back up the trail. So, she had been supporting her worthless brother.

I'd been mulling over Decker's news for a few minutes when Harper called out to me. "What are you doing down there?"

"Watching the ocean. On my way back up."

"Let me come to you instead." Harper reached down, took off her heels, and walked barefoot. "It is so beautiful here," she said, sitting down on my lap rather than on the bench.

"It is that."

"I take it that was bad news."

"At least I have some idea of the motivation behind my uncle's behavior."

"Money?"

"How did you guess?"

"Recent experience. It makes people do stupid things. Take Dave, for example. I didn't have that much money when we got engaged. My dad liked him and, I guess, wanted me to marry him, so he offered to pay for a lot of the wedding. Not all of it, but more than half. Dave said his parents had offered to cover the rest. It wasn't extravagant by any means. My way of thinking, we were two kids right out of college; why waste a bunch of money on a wedding? And yet, he ran up what became 'our' credit cards and emptied our bank account."

"You've been trying to figure out why he did it."

"Wouldn't you?"

"Absolutely. I'm just relieved that you let go of the notion of returning any money to him."

Harper's brow furrowed.

"You have given up on that, yes?"

"I suppose."

"Glad to hear it."

"The thing that makes no sense to me is why he said he'd get even with me. All I did, or all Decker did, was retrieve my money. How can you get even with someone for reclaiming what you stole?"

"It didn't stop there, Harper."

"What do you mean?"

"Certain arrangements put into place may have made his life somewhat difficult."

She got off my lap and sat on the bench. "What arrangements?"

"Nothing he didn't deserve, Harper. Your hands were tied in terms of pressing charges against him. You comingled your finances, so there were no means to determine what money in the account belonged to him or to you."

She folded her arms.

"He was let go from his job when his employer discovered evidence that he was embezzling money."

"Was he?"

"Perhaps not to the extent the evidence indicated." I didn't know for certain, but it wouldn't be unlike Decker to pad the proof.

"What else?"

"More of the same."

"Saint."

"There are certain things about him you don't need to know, Harper. Trust me on this. It will only serve to hurt you."

"What?"

The last thing I wanted to do was cause her pain, but she deserved to know the full extent of her ex's betrayal. I sighed. "You weren't the only woman he was involved with."

"Was he going to marry her too?"

"It appears so. Although not just one."

"Oh my God. I can't believe this!"

"I need to ask. Are you angry with me over your slimeball ex-fiancé getting what was his due?"

"Why didn't you tell me?" She studied me.

"I can assure you I didn't personally facilitate any of this. In fact, I would've preferred to stay ignorant of the details."

Harper looked out at the ocean and didn't say anything for a time. Finally, she let out a heavy sigh. "I felt like something was off. I didn't want to admit it to myself, but I noticed. It always seemed like he was holding something back. The fact that he reminded me of my dad should've been enough for me to end the relationship."

"Why didn't you?"

"I was about to graduate from college. The degree I'd worked so hard for seemed, at the time, a dead end in terms of the kind of work I wanted to do. I was disillusioned with the overall state of ministry, and the jobs I did see posted were for positions I'd never want to take. Dave was the picture-perfect boyfriend. He was attentive and sweet to me. I didn't have a lot of friends, but he did, so they became mine too. And he didn't pressure me into having sex, even after we were engaged."

I did my best to stifle a groan, hearing his name and sex mentioned so closely together.

"I was going through the motions, Saint. I blame myself as much as him."

"Going through the motions and stealing someone's money are two very different things, Harper. You have no blame in this."

She shook her head. "I'm sorry. You were telling me about your uncle, and I made the conversation all about me."

"What do you say we forget about everything besides enjoying each other and celebrating Rile and Kensington's wedding tomorrow?"

There would be plenty of time once we were back in London for me to deal with my mother's brother.

We saw more of the Invincibles team the next morning when we came downstairs for breakfast at the inn Rile had bought out for the wedding guests.

"Good morning, Saint," said Z Alexander.

"Z. May I present Harper Godfrey?"

"Ah, yes, I've heard a great deal about you."

"And I, you." Her cheeks flushed pink, but since she didn't drop her gaze, I was able to stave off tossing her over my shoulder and taking her back to our room.

"I've also heard you made it official with IISG."

I smiled, preferring the acronym far more than the shortened version of the name of the organization.

"Yes, I did."

"I'm happy for you, Saint. I do believe it's a better fit for you. Although, I'm not looking forward to hearing from your uncle about you not rejoining MI6."

"Yes, well…"

Z studied me.

"If there's something I need to know, spit it out."

"Given your close personal relationship with Decker, he may be better suited to pass on whatever information he's unearthed."

The man himself entered the dining area moments later, accompanied by Mila and their baby.

Z stood when they approached. "Come here and see your grandpa," he said, holding out his hands to the boy, who went willingly. Z sat and bounced the baby on his lap. "I understand your dada has some information he's been withholding from me," he said in a singsong voice.

Decker shot me a glare.

"Don't look at him, son. I was lamenting the wrath I would face once the foreign secretary learned I'd failed to get his nephew to return to his former position with MI6."

"You had no intention of rehiring him," said Decker.

Z nodded. "For his own good." He turned to me. "I'm not quite as unaware as you may think."

I laughed. "I would never accuse you of being so. Baiting, yes. Unaware, no."

I looked over at Harper, who had been chatting with Mila. Now, though, she was studying something on her phone.

"Everything okay?"

"It isn't. Reverend Primrose is in the hospital."

I stood, helped with her chair, and led her out to the inn's foyer. "How serious is his condition?"

"He's scheduled for surgery tomorrow."

"We'll catch the first flight out in the morning. Unless you'd rather leave this evening."

Harper raised her brow. "We will? And, no, I don't want to miss the wedding."

"I've kept you away from your new role as his assistant too long as it is."

Harper put her phone in her handbag and her arms around my waist. "Thank you, Saint."

Decker joined us in the foyer.

"I'll let you two talk," Harper said when she spotted him.

"More on my uncle's dastardly ways?"

"News on Dr. Benjamin."

His tone worried me. "And?"

"We think we've located him. Not just Adam, his son too."

This was big news. Jinyan Tai Man had disappeared nine years ago, and we weren't the only ones looking for him. "Where?"

"The Sundarbans."

"India or Bangladesh?" A little over half the national park was in the former, the rest in the latter.

Decker raised a brow. It was a ridiculous question, given the relationship between India and China was rife with tension, particularly over their inability to come to a border agreement.

Bangladesh, on the other hand, had been working overtime to develop a relationship with the superpower intent on making the twenty-first century the Asian century.

As a place to hide, it was quite brilliant. Far in the jungle and hours from a single established village—and that was only by boat—it was home to the world's largest mangrove forests as well as several hundred Bengal tigers. Most importantly, its actual distance from China might be relatively short, but it was worlds away politically.

"Getting there is a challenge," said Decker. "You'll fly into Dumdum, Kolkata, and then arrange for a boat to take you into the tiger reserve."

"That's where they are?"

Decker smiled. "One mission I'm glad I won't be on. At least not on the ground."

"Arsehole," I muttered under my breath. "Do we have any reason to believe Benjamin and Jinyan will be relocating in the next few days?"

"Looks to me that Tai Man has been settled there for months if not years."

"In the tiger reserve? How is that even legal? You're not shitting me?"

This time he laughed. "You're not firing with all cylinders if you're suggesting Jinyan would care about legalities, and I'm sure as shit not shitting you."

"How quickly can we assemble a team?"

"Rip is on his way to London now. We've got a few hours before the wedding to figure out who else to send in. Let's get Z involved. He'll want MI6 to get at least part of the credit for bringing in Jinyan. That also means funding."

"Thanks, Decker. I appreciate this."

"It's what we do, Saint."

This was the most inopportune time to be on the island of Mallorca with everything I had to arrange both for Harper and myself.

First up was making sure she could stay at Fox Run Cottage. I walked outside and placed a call to the one person I thought would be able to facilitate it most easily.

27

Harper

I watched as Decker came back into the dining room and Saint walked outside. Mila looked up at her husband, who took the baby from her arms and sat at the table with us.

What I found most surprising was that she didn't ask a single question about what he and Saint had been discussing or if everything was okay. I had to bite the inside of my cheek to stop myself from doing so.

"Saint, Z, and I will need some time to meet this morning," Decker said, looking from me to his wife.

"Okay," she murmured. "I should grab something to eat now, then. Harper, you haven't ordered yet, have you?"

I hadn't, although I was hungry, and said so.

Since I had no idea when Saint would come back in, or if he'd have time to order and eat before their meeting, I ordered extra food when the waiter came to our table. Shortly after I'd done so, Saint motioned to me from the foyer; he must've come in when I wasn't looking.

"Hi," I said, stopping myself from asking the questions Mila hadn't asked her husband.

I expected him to speak. Instead, he led me over to an alcove and put his arms around me, shattering my resolve not to ask questions I shouldn't.

"Is everything okay?"

"It will be." Saint rested his head on mine and sighed. "The next several days are going to be complicated."

"If it is a problem for me to go to Alfriston, it's okay, Saint. I don't want to make things harder on you."

"Not at all, actually. That part is quite easy." He cleared his throat. "Apart from the vicar's health, of course."

He brought his lips to mine in the sweetest, softest kiss. It almost brought me to tears. What was he trying to tell me? I felt something significant. "Saint?"

"I've made arrangements for Eliza to meet us at Fox Run Cottage. She'll stay there with you until I return."

"I'm not supposed to ask where you're going, am I?"

"You are not. And worse, I'm not allowed to confide anything in you."

"This will be how our life is." It was a statement, not a question. I'd agreed to marry Saint, and with that came both his responsibilities and mine.

"We'll talk more later," he said when we saw Decker and Z walk into the foyer from the dining room. He kissed me one more time before leading me out of the alcove.

28

Saint

Eliza had promised me her father would not give her or Harper any grief while they were in Alfriston.

"I'll hold you to that vow," I said before ringing off. While I had enough on Nigel to threaten him into good behavior myself, I doubted I'd have the time to do it.

I knew Harper was worried, and tonight, after the wedding, I'd do what I could to assuage her.

"Who do you want from SIS?" Z asked when I went upstairs to his suite to meet.

"Who's left?" I asked.

"Not many, thanks to him." Z pointed at Decker.

Decker smirked and then softened the look on his face. "We have plenty we can pull in. Rip is on his way. There's Ink. He'd come in handy with the tigers."

Breckin "Ink" Ryan was the *biggest* man I'd ever known. Not only in height, but also in bulk. The man had the largest, most defined muscles I'd ever seen outside of a movie. When other agents accused him of taking steroids to achieve his mass, he offered to take a drug test to prove them wrong. I'd asked him at the time why the accusation didn't make him angry.

"I hear it at least once a week. Getting in a snit about it would only serve to make the person asking more suspicious."

"Yes on Ink," I said, studying the website and looking for availability. One name jumped out at me, and not because I wanted him on this mission.

"Do you think Hammer could assist in figuring out the legality of the cottage's title?" Sterling "Hammer" Anderson was the Invincibles' attorney and was accustomed to flying around the globe when he was needed, even if only for his opinion in places where he wasn't licensed to practice law.

There was actually something else entirely I wanted to discuss with him and put into place before I left for India, but it wasn't something I intended to talk to anyone but Hammer about.

"Sure," said Decker. "Let him earn his retainer for once. Who else?"

We went through the list and came up with two additional names: Mick "Jagger" Reynolds and Ritter "Rock" Johnson. Both men had worked extensively with Rip, which would make the three of them a good team.

"We'll have Crash on transport. If he needs a copilot, we can pull Angel in," said Decker.

Smith "Crash" Lavery was an American; Teagon "Angel" Evans, a Brit. I knew both quite well. In fact, I'd heard there was an ongoing dalliance between them.

"Now that we have that settled, let's figure out how to get you in there."

"Here's what I want to know," said Z. "What do we do with Jinyan once we get him out?"

"How badly do you want him?" Decker asked.

"You would think out of loyalty alone, you'd just hand him over."

Quite honestly, I didn't care what happened to Adam Benjamin's son. No one, whether it was MI6 or the CIA, would want him for more than the level of intelligence he would bring with him, even if only in his head.

Benjamin himself was a different story. If our mission was successful, I'd be giving him what he wanted, and the debt—that I'd imposed and carried—would be wiped out. I'd sternly warn him that if he chose to go back to Hong Kong or China in the future, I wouldn't be going in after him.

"You good with that, Saint?" asked Decker.

"I'm sorry, what?"

"I told you he wasn't paying attention," he said to Z.

"I don't give a rat's arse what happens to Jinyan, if that's what you're referring to."

"What about Dr. Benjamin?" Z asked.

"Strip him of his passport and ensure he never gets another."

Both men laughed, but I was deadly serious.

"If we're done here, I'd like some time with my wife and son before the wedding."

"I'll convene with the team once they all arrive in London, and we'll craft our plan," I told both men, standing to leave when Decker did.

"Saint, can you spare another minute?" Z asked.

"Of course." I sat back down and followed the man's line of sight. Pride flowed from his eyes.

"Did you ever think Decker would settle down and get married?" I asked.

"I'm more surprised that he agreed to run the Invincibles."

"I didn't realize he was running it. I thought there were several managing partners responsible for different parts of the world."

"If you think Deck doesn't have his hands in every mission the team undertakes, you're not as smart as I've always believed you to be."

"What do you wish to discuss?"

"Your uncle."

I wasn't surprised in the least. "What are your thoughts, Z?"

"We can go one of two ways. Scandal or no scandal. Quite honestly, I think he deserves to have his name dragged through a bit of dirt, but that reflects on you, Saint. And the rest of your family."

Funny how the tables had turned. For years, Nigel had berated me for my "inappropriate lifestyle." Now, his life was a sham, a house of cards that would soon crumble. As with many things of late, I found myself wondering what Harper would do.

"If you don't mind, I'll get back to you on that, Z."

"We won't be able to keep his financial mess a secret long, Saint."

"Understood."

I left the room in search of Harper. Our meeting hadn't lasted terribly long, so I returned to the dining room. When she saw me, her face broke into a smile complete with the dimples I adored. I leaned down and kissed her cheek.

"I ordered extra in case you were hungry," she said, pointing to the plates in front of her. "They probably thought I was a glutton."

"Thank you for that. I am quite famished." I sat beside her and pierced a piece of melon with my fork. "There are a few things I'd like to discuss with you. Back in the room."

"Okay." Her cheeks flushed, and her gaze dropped.

"Well, now that you've done that, I doubt I'll be able to remember anything I planned to discuss."

The look on Harper's face was full of heat and want, mirroring my own thoughts.

"What about the wedding?" she asked when, a few hours later, she tried to get up, but I pulled her back in bed.

"Right. I suppose we should make an appearance."

Harper laughed, wriggled out of my grasp, and went into the lavatory. I heard the shower go on and was about to join her when a feeling of melancholy came over me.

Three days from now, maybe four, I would bid farewell to the woman who made my heart sing. Like with being unable to confide in her, I'd never experienced leaving someone I loved, without being able to say with absolute certainty that I'd be back.

What that would do to Harper was more than I could think about. I wondered how someone like Decker did it. It wasn't just his wife; now they had a baby, who would be left fatherless if a mission went wrong.

The ache in my chest was too great for me to allow myself to continue thinking about it, especially given we'd soon be attending a joyous wedding. I rolled my body out of bed, hoping I still had time to run my hands over Harper's naked, wet body.

I'd told Harper the King and Queen of Spain would be in attendance, but based on the lack of security entering the estate, I wondered if they'd changed their mind. As long as Kensington showed up, I was sure Rile wouldn't care a whit. And vice versa.

I wondered if Harper was thinking similar thoughts. I hadn't stopped to consider attending a wedding might be difficult for her.

"I can't imagine a more beautiful setting," she commented when we came out of the forest and the view opened to the Balearic Sea.

The sun shone brightly today, and the sky was a perfect blue, just like the reflection in the pond the first day we'd visited Alfriston.

We were dropped off right in front of the small chapel that had been on the estate for a hundred years. It was new in comparison to the one where Harper would be ministering, but no less enchanting.

We had just taken our places near the back on the groom's side when a hush came over the chapel.

I recognized the Spanish royalty, but not because they were in their regalia. There was just something about the way they held themselves that set them apart.

Until they stopped at the front pew and greeted the woman sitting on the bride's side, I hadn't realized it was the Queen. Again, she wore simple attire and looked like she could be Kensington's grandmother.

"Oh my gosh," said Harper, putting her hand in front of her mouth. "That's her, isn't it?"

"I believe it is."

I was stunned when her eyes filled with tears.

"What is it, my darling?" Was it the memory of her own wedding that brought her to tears?

"Everything is so beautiful. Simple, yet perfect. I would love our wedding to be like this. That's if you wouldn't mind."

"As I'm sure Rile would say about Kensington, you will be all that matters to me the day you become my wife. I love you, Harper."

"I love you, Saint."

The music changed, the congregation stood, and the bride's processional began.

After a short but very moving service, we exited the pews and were greeted by the bride and groom when we reached the door.

"It was a lovely wedding," I heard Harper say to Kensington as my eyes met Rile's. When she stepped in front of him, he took her left hand and kissed the back of it.

"It is an honor to meet the woman who has captured Saint's heart." Rile was one of my closest and dearest friends, and his graciousness moved me.

We shook when it was my turn, before Rile pulled me into an embrace. "She is the one, my friend. Never doubt it. You will live a long and happy life with her by your side."

Some said Rile had a sixth sense. I'd certainly seen it in action in the years I'd known him. This time, though, I prayed what he'd seen came to fruition.

"Godspeed," he said, releasing me.

"And to you."

"Saint," he called after me. "Keep your eye on the tiger's."

I shuddered at his words, knowing without any doubt that Decker had not shared the details of our upcoming mission with him. None of us wanted Rile's mind to be on anything other than his bride.

29

Harper

I'd said so many prayers today, I lost track. Not that I ever really kept count. I could tell from Saint's demeanor—along with Decker's and some of the other guys'—that whatever they were about to do was dangerous.

"Please keep him safe. Please, God, bring him back to me."

It was selfish, but I couldn't help it. Niven St. Thomas had changed my life. He'd changed me. I'd never felt more alive than I had since we met on the plane. I couldn't allow myself to envision my future without him.

"Come here," he said, leading me over to the bed when we returned to our room after the reception's festivities ended. "We're going to talk, Harper, and then we are going to make love until we fall asleep in each other's arms."

I shook my head. "I don't want to talk, Saint." The words were impossible to speak without crying.

"We must, my darling. There are things you need to know. There's also something I want to ask you."

I rolled my shoulders, wiped my tears, and sat beside him on the bed.

"A man will be meeting us in Alfriston tomorrow. His name is Sterling Anderson, and the purpose of his visit is to ensure that if anything were to happen to me, you will be taken care of for the rest of your life."

I had no control over the tears that streamed down my cheeks. "I don't want anything, Saint. I don't want to be taken care of. I only want you."

"And I, you, my darling. Please understand I'm doing this for my own peace of mind. I beg you to indulge me."

I wiped my tears, took a deep breath, and let it out slowly. "Eliza said your uncle tried to control you."

He nodded and smiled.

"And then she said there wasn't a man less likely to allow it."

"Are you saying you're acquiescing?"

I stared into his blue eyes and let my gaze linger on his beautiful face. Why a man like him would want to be with someone like me rather than with a supermodel baffled me. But he did. And he loved me. Of that, I had no doubt. "Would my protests do any good?"

He grinned. "Not even a little."

"Then, I won't bother."

"If that's the case, I've one more request."

Not only was Saint handsome, but he could charm the dew off the honeysuckle, as my grandmother used to say. "Don't push it, Saint."

He took both my hands in his, and the grin left his face. "Before I leave, I want you to marry me. Be my wife."

I choked on the breath I'd just taken and sobbed my words in response. *"Why? No. Why are you doing this?"* Every part of me hurt at knowing what was behind this. Saint believed he might not come back. "You begged me to give in earlier. To indulge you. Now I'm begging you not to ask this."

"Harper, I don't want anyone to attempt to contest my will. If you are my wife, that cannot happen."

"It still can, Saint, and I have no doubt your uncle would fight me to…" I couldn't continue. I couldn't talk about death. Only love.

"I will meet with him before I leave. I wasn't certain I'd have time, but I'll make it. During our meeting, I'll extend him an offer I am most certain he'll accept. In doing so, he will relinquish all claims to my estate, and he will allow you to live in Fox Run Cottage for the rest of your life—or as long as you want."

I put my head in my hands and prayed out loud. "God, I beg you to keep Niven safe. Keep my husband safe and allow us to spend our lives together here on earth and, one day, when we are very old, together in heaven. Amen."

Saint's eyes opened wide, and his hold on my hands tightened. "Does this mean you agree? You know, of course, that we can still have a traditional wedding later. However, wherever, you want. This is only for us. You and me."

"I will agree, but I have a condition."

"Name it."

"This is the last time we'll speak of such things until we are with the lawyer and the man who will marry us. Once they both know your wishes, we will not talk about it again before you leave."

"I give you my word." He looked up at the ceiling. "In front of God."

"Good. Now, you promised we would make love until we fall asleep in each other's arms."

"A vow I am very happy to honor."

With the number of guests leaving Mallorca today, Saint and I said our goodbyes without telling anyone we were flying back to London. Neither of us wanted a private plane arranged for us. In fact, we were giddy that we'd be flying first class together again.

"Can I get you anything to drink?" the flight attendant asked Saint. He raised our hands that were clasped together in such a way that the woman couldn't help but see my ring.

"My wife and I would like two cracks of champagne if you would, please."

"We aren't married *yet*." I giggled when she walked away.

"*You* started it when you called me husband." Saint's expression changed from silly to serious. "But aren't we, Harper? In the eyes of God, aren't we already man and wife? Weren't we the night we consecrated our union?"

I nodded solemnly. "You're right."

His face broke into his movie-star-like smile. "Besides, I can't stop myself from saying it."

We'd agreed this morning that, after he dropped me off at the flat, Saint would go and talk with his uncle on his own. It was fine by me. Whatever they had to say to each other, I didn't want to know.

Now that Saint was a partner in the Invincibles, he no longer had to kowtow to Nigel or even listen to his demands, and for that, I gave a prayer of thanks.

"Hello? Miss Bardwell?" Saint called out when the elevator opened on the foyer of his flat.

"I'm here," she shouted, coming around the corner from the hallway.

My left hand hung at my side, and she raced over and grabbed it.

"Oh, thank the heavens! It is a *perfect* fit. The *perfect* ring for the *perfect* woman." Her eyes filled with tears, and she cupped both our cheeks. "May God bless you. You have brought my heart such joy."

Saint winked at me, and I smiled at him.

He carried our bags down the hallway and into the bedroom. I followed to freshen up.

"I'm off, then," he said when I came out of the bathroom. "The sooner I do this, the sooner I'll be back."

While he was gone, I made three phone calls. First to my mother, then to my father, and finally to Mouse. I'd left her until last, knowing I would likely need to vent or cry or something after talking to my parents.

My mother, once she recovered from the shock, cried tears of joy, making me promise Saint and I would visit her in the States as soon as we could.

My father reacted in the exact way I expected him to. "This is absurd, Harper," he said rather than "Congratulations!" or "I'm so happy for you, my beloved daughter!" Not that he'd ever used any of those words when talking to or about me. I couldn't help but wonder if he'd change his tune after our phone call ended, and he researched his future son-in-law. I predicted it would.

"I knew it!" proclaimed Mouse after I admitted fibbing to her when I told her I was staying with a man I met on the plane and his wife.

I laughed. "That's ridiculous. How could you know?"

"There's something in your voice I've never heard before. You sound different. Happy. At peace. I can picture you glowing like an angel."

I couldn't admit it to Mouse—because I hadn't told Saint yet—but I had an overwhelming feeling that I was pregnant. There were no signs of it, no symptoms, yet in my heart, I knew I was.

We ended the call with me promising to be in touch about our plans for a wedding, not the one that would happen in the next day or two, but the wedding we would share with those we loved. The one we'd plan when Saint returned from his mission.

"Please, God," I prayed out loud. "Let him come back from his mission."

30

Saint

"Come in, Niven," said my uncle when he answered my knock at his door. He ushered me into the sitting room, the same one where he'd disparaged both Harper and me. The memory of it made me angry enough to rethink my offer to him; however, my intended outcome kept me steadfast.

"Where is Millicent?" I asked.

"Out with friends. Shopping or some sort of thing. But never mind that. Are you here to tell me you've had a change of heart? Are you and the American planning to announce your engagement? Once you have, I'll set the wheels in motion for you to return to MI6."

It was sad, really, that my uncle believed he wielded that kind of power when, in reality, he wasn't important enough to be kept abreast of how many things had transpired that would go against his plan.

"On the contrary, Uncle. I've come to discuss another matter entirely."

The pompous ass smirked. "And what would that be?"

"The matter of your role as foreign secretary and whether you are willing to go along with my demands in order to remain in the position."

His beady eyes scrunched, and the tone of his voice became menacing—or it might have been to someone who didn't know they held all the cards. "Enough games, Niven. Tell me your intentions or leave. If you walk out that door, you'll no longer receive any assistance from me whatsoever."

"Assistance from *you*? What a joke! You can't manage to keep your own affairs in order, let alone those of anyone else. That you believe you influence *anything* is the biggest joke of all."

"I beg your pardon?" he bellowed, rising from the chair. I stood as well and stared him down.

"We both know the financial mess you're in, so let's stop with the charade. What I don't understand is why you didn't come to me in the first place."

He cleared his throat and walked over to pour himself a drink. He didn't offer me one. "I've no idea what you're talking about."

I withdrew the papers I'd brought from my inside jacket pocket, walked over, and handed them to him.

"What is the meaning of this?" he asked, staring down at the first page.

"Enough, Uncle!" I bellowed like he had. "I have little time and even less patience. Are you prepared to listen to my offer, or shall I walk out and leave you to your own devices?"

There were many other things I thought to say, all of them as disparaging as what he'd said to me over the course of most of my adult life. However, all it took to soothe me was closing my eyes and picturing my darling Harper.

"I cannot wait to hear this."

I reined in the flare of my temper brought on by his snide tone. "First, I am prepared to give you the funds you need to pay off your debts."

His eyes opened wide. "In exchange for *what*?"

I smiled. This is where it would get good. "I have several requirements." I motioned to the dining room table, sat when he did, and pulled another set of papers from my opposite jacket pocket. "First, let's talk about

Fox Run Cottage." I set the papers in front of him. "As you can see, and as you well know, it is not within your rights to sell. If you wish to deny your inheritance, the terms of the title decree that you first make offer of it to the remaining heirs. If either, in this case, wish to take over the property, you must relinquish it to them."

"*Relinquish it? Never.* It's worth close to a million pounds."

I set another paper in front of him. "And, as you can also see, Eliza has signed over her claim to the property. I, however, am prepared to take possession of it."

"I will not agree to this." He spoke far more quietly than he had to this point. "I cannot."

"As *I* well know, which is why I am also prepared to pay you the million pounds you believe is the cottage's fair market value. A sum quite close to the total amount of your debt."

He looked from the paper up to me. "And what are you asking of me in exchange?"

"First, you give up this flat. You and Millicent may choose any other within the budget I set for you. I assure you, the two of you will live out your days quite comfortably, although not *extravagantly*."

"You would turn us out of our home?"

I took a deep breath and let it out slowly. "A home my mother purchased *for* you and which you have mortgaged to within a penny of its worth. Which means you will not have the money to continue residing here."

"Where would you have us go?"

"As I said, you will have the choice. One of the stipulations is that your purchase remains within the budget I set."

He sneered. "What are the other *stipulations*?"

"That home will remain in your daughter's name and mine in order to prevent you from mortgaging it as you did this one. Upon your death and that of your wife, Eliza will inherit the property free and clear. Let me assure you, any plans you may have to manipulate her, will result in my turning you out in the street."

His face turned red. "What else?" He glared with hooded eyes.

"You will live within the means afforded to you by your salary as foreign secretary."

"But that's—"

"My final offer. You will note I am allowing you to remain in the position you hold in such high regard.

That can easily change, Uncle. Where do you think I came by all of this information? I'll answer for you. *MI6.* And I promise you, Z Alexander is prepared to open a formal inquiry and see to it you are stripped from your appointment."

He sat back in his chair, but it was easy to see he was attempting to come up with a different plan. I pushed my chair away and stood. "Every hour that passes without you signing the documents I have given you, the budget for your future home decreases by one hundred thousand pounds. I'd make haste if I were you." I turned to leave.

"Wait, Niven!" he called out to me before I reached his front door. "I'll sign."

"Excellent decision."

"Before I do, what exactly is the budget?"

"Five hundred thousand pounds."

"You can't touch anything anywhere near this neighborhood for less than three times that sum."

"No, Uncle, you cannot."

I watched as he signed and dated each document.

"I'll have my solicitor forward copies to you by the end of the week. You will have thirty days to find another home. Once escrow begins, its close will become the deadline by which you must vacate this flat."

"Since your parents died, I have treated you like a son. I cannot believe you would thank me in such a way."

"Since my parents died, you have treated me as a hired hand, Nigel. The respect I afforded you in return you did not deserve, yet I gave it anyway. I think what you meant to say instead was, 'Thank you, Niven.'"

I waited, but he did not speak.

"As I expected." I sighed. "My solicitor will be in touch."

When I returned to the flat, Harper was sitting in a chair by the window, reading. The sight replenished the joy I'd lost in visiting my uncle.

"Are you sure you want to make the drive to Alfriston this afternoon?" she asked when I leaned down to kiss her cheek.

"Very much so. Any word on the vicar?"

"His surgery went quite well. It was his gallbladder, and according to Mrs. Rippington, it is possible to remove it through a person's belly button." She cringed and scrunched her shoulders.

"Mrs. Rippington?"

"Your neighbor at Fox Run. You know, Barbara's mother?"

I didn't recall the Rippington name at all and wouldn't have put it together with Barbara, given her last name was Walters. "Good news, then, right?"

"Very good. The vicar called shortly after I talked to your neighbor. He said he should be home tomorrow but will not be visiting parishes for at least three weeks."

"Will you be going in his place?" I could predict the answer by the look on her lovely face.

Harper beamed, then worried her lip. "I will be, but…"

"Driving?"

"Yes. How did you know? I mean, I know how to drive, but I don't have a car, and then I'll have to learn to do it on the opposite side." She shuddered. "I'll figure it out, though."

I held out my hand and when she took it, helped her out of the chair and over to the sofa, where I pulled her close and wrapped her in my arms. "As I told you before, Eliza will be with you the entire time I'm away. Once I return, I'll take over as your chauffeur." I kissed her cheek. "What else is worrying you, Harper?"

"You leaving, of course."

"And?"

She sighed. "I talked to Mouse today. She said Dave was asking around about me, mainly where I was."

"Apart from the fact no one knows, unless you've told them, would anyone who did, divulge such information to the daft-wit?"

That made her laugh. "I doubt it. Except maybe my dad." She rested her head on my shoulder. "I talked to him today too."

I knew instantly by her tone that it hadn't been a pleasant conversation. If I ever had the displeasure of meeting the wanker, he'd get an earful from me about the way he treated his daughter.

Would that I could take away her hurt. Instead, I'd spend every day of my life making sure she knew I loved her.

"My mom is happy for us. She can't wait to meet you."

"You were busy while I was away." While I hated to sour her mood, we needed to circle back to her concern about her ex. "As much as I would prefer to forget his existence, tell me why your ex asking about you has you worried."

Harper shrugged. "He sounded so *mean* the day he called."

"I can assure you he doesn't have the *means* to act on his words." That brought a smile to her face.

"I know. Talking to Mouse just reminded me of a time of my life I'd rather forget."

"I worried a bit about how you'd feel at the wedding." I hadn't planned to mention it to her, but decided the more we talked about it, the sooner she could put it behind her. Plus, we had our own wedding to discuss.

"I was worried too, but once we arrived, I didn't give it another thought. Maybe if it had taken place at the same church ours was supposed to, it might have bothered me more. Or even on the same continent."

I checked the time and saw we'd have to leave soon if we wanted to get to the cottage before Eliza, who had agreed to pick Hammer up from Heathrow and bring him to Alfriston.

"We should be on our way, my darling."

"I'm ready." She wriggled from my arms, stood, and held her hand out to me. "Come on, let's go!"

I laughed. "You're suddenly anxious."

"Not suddenly. You'll never have to ask twice about going to Alfriston. I feel so at home there."

I hadn't yet told her about the deal I made with my uncle or that if she wanted it, Alfriston and Fox Run *would* be her home.

31

Harper

I couldn't tear my eyes away from the scenery during the drive from London to Alfriston. I would whisper the names of the towns we passed through as if by saying them, I could declare my intent to visit one day.

There was Thornton Heath, Netherne-on-the-Hill, Crawley, Pease Pottage—which made me giggle—Smallfield, and Lowfield Heath, among countless others.

Saint seemed as lost in thought as I was. I liked that we could be together without either of us feeling the need to fill the peacefulness and tranquility of the silence with unnecessary words.

We hadn't talked about when exactly we'd get married or who would perform the service. I both cared and didn't. As Saint had said, all that mattered was that he and I would be there. We would say our vows and commit our lives to each other. I would've liked our union to be consecrated, but I knew in my heart that God looked down on us with his favor.

Saint reached over, took my hand, and brought it to his lips. "You soothe me, my darling Harper. Your presence alone brings peace to my soul," he said as though he knew I'd come to my own peace over our wedding.

"You do the same for me."

"I fear you are just being kind. You wouldn't, though, would you? Lie, I mean."

"Not to you. Not about how I feel about you."

He kissed my hand again, but when he lowered it, he didn't let go. "Not much farther."

"I know," I sighed.

When we pulled in front of the cottage, I couldn't believe my eyes. Someone had cleared the overgrowth from the garden. While it looked sparse, I could clearly see its beauty come spring when the plants would no longer be dormant.

I rested my hand on my belly, wondering if the baby I knew was growing inside me would be a boy or a girl. Either way, I could envision Saint, me, and however many children God blessed us with, tending this garden and this home with love.

Worry crept in, but each time it did, I closed my eyes and pictured our family.

"Everything okay?" Saint asked, looking down to where my hand rested.

"Everything is wonderful."

He raised a brow. "Harper?"

"You'll think I'm daft." I smiled, using the word he so often did.

He leaned over and put his hand on mine.

"I'm pregnant. I know it's far too early to know medically, but I am."

"I thought to ask," he whispered.

"You did? Why?"

"There is a glow about you. You remain the loveliest woman I've ever seen, but over the last couple of days…I can't explain it. I thought perhaps it was because we would soon be wed, but I like the idea of you being pregnant far more."

"Me too." I pointed at the garden. "Did you arrange for this?"

"I would like to take credit, but no. I think perhaps Eliza may have had something to do with it."

It wouldn't have surprised me a bit if it had been him. Saint's words the day we met on the plane, echoed in my mind. "You, Harper, deserve to be with a man who will hold you in the highest regard, love you endlessly, and make it his life's mission to do everything in his power to keep this lovely smile on your face."

He was that man, and I knew he would honor that unspoken vow along with the others we would soon make.

When he moved our hands, leaned down, and kissed my belly, my eyes filled with tears. He didn't doubt me. He believed I was pregnant too.

When he sat up, something in the rearview mirror caught his attention. "They're here," he said, waving behind him. I made a move to open my door, but Saint put his hand on my arm. "Allow me, please."

I sat and waited while he hurried around, opened my door, and held his hand out to me. I looked into his beautiful eyes and smiled when he said, "Welcome home, my darling."

I turned to look at the cottage I'd fallen as much in love with as I had Saint. I so wished this could be our home. However, as much as I wanted it to be, it wasn't worth Saint having to succumb to his uncle's wishes.

While Saint said hello to the man who exited the other car, Eliza approached and cheek-kissed me.

"Are you responsible for all this?" I asked, motioning with my head toward the garden.

"I'd like to take credit, but my understanding is the vicar, Reverend Primrose, along with the neighbor, Mrs. Rippington, arranged for several of Alfriston's residents to come over and prepare the cottage for your impending arrival."

"Perhaps it was more to prepare it for sale."

Eliza shrugged and turned toward the men when Saint approached. "Harper, this is my dear friend Sterling Anderson, who most call Hammer. Hammer, this is the love of my life and soon to be Mrs. St. Thomas, Harper."

Like Rile had at the wedding, Hammer took my outstretched hand and kissed the back of it. "It's an honor to meet you, miss."

"Wait. Are you American?"

"Texas born and bred."

"Shall we go inside?" Saint asked, opening the gate that led into the garden.

"Eliza said Reverend Primrose and Mrs. Rippington were responsible for all this." I waved my hands on either side of the walkway.

"You don't say," Saint said with a wink, letting me know he was in on it after all.

"If you'd give us a moment," he said to Eliza and Hammer when we reached the front door. He opened it, swept me into his arms, and carried me over the threshold.

When he set me on my feet and I turned around, I gasped. Some of the old furniture had been replaced while many of the antiques remained. Everywhere I could see had a fresh coat of paint, and the place looked as though it had been cleaned from the ceiling to the floor. Bouquets of flowers were on several of the tables. "What is all this?" I asked.

"When I said 'welcome home,' I meant it, Harper. Fox Run is ours now."

I studied him. "What do you mean?"

"It is my wedding gift to my beautiful soon-to-be bride."

I didn't care how it had happened; I was too happy it had. I threw my arms around Saint's neck and kissed him.

"Ahem." Hammer cleared his throat. "You have more visitors."

I looked behind him and Eliza, through the door, and saw Mrs. Rippington pushing a wheelchair occupied by Reverend Primose.

"Oh my goodness," I shouted, rushing out to greet them. "How are you even out of the hospital?"

"Pishposh," said the vicar. "'Twas nothing but a minor inconvenience. The doctors are making far too much of it."

I looked up at Mrs. Rippington, who rolled her eyes and winked.

"Let me help," said Saint, rushing out like I had.

"If you've got this, I'll be on my way. Just give me a holler when he's ready to go," said the woman.

"Thank you," I said after her, and she waved.

"Come now, you two," said the vicar. "I understand we've a wedding here today."

Like they always did, my eyes filled with tears, but this time, I couldn't see to walk. I felt Saint's arms go around me, and he carried me inside like he had only a few minutes ago. When he set me on my feet for the second time, I saw Hammer had wheeled the vicar in.

"While we'll still take care of the other things we discussed, the vicar suggested we do first things first and be married," Saint said to me.

"Come with me," said Eliza, taking my hand, leading me into the bedroom, and closing the door behind us. "While you are the perfect picture of a beautiful bride, there's something I want to show you. If you don't want to wear it, you don't have to." She walked over to the closet, opened the door, and pulled out a silk wedding gown. I gasped.

"This belonged to Saint's mother, Margaret. When she died, Saint found it stored in the back of a closet in his flat. He'd intended to get rid of it, but I begged him to let me have it."

"It's so beautiful." I reached out and touched the cream-colored fabric.

"It looks to me like it will fit you perfectly."

"I'd love to wear it," I said when I noticed Eliza staring at me, her hands clasped as if in prayer.

"I can step out if you'd like."

"Would you mind helping me get into it? I'd hate to rip it or anything."

"I'd be honored."

32

"Where'd they run off to?" I asked Hammer when several minutes passed without either Harper or Eliza coming out of the bedroom.

"It's her wedding, man. Don't rush her." He nudged me with this elbow.

"Thanks for making the trip, my friend."

"I'd say it's what the Invincibles pay me for, but the truth is, I wouldn't have missed this day for anything in the world."

The door opened, and my cousin walked out first. Her tear-filled eyes met mine.

"She's so beautiful," she whispered.

I saw her then. My angel. My darling. My Harper. My eyes—filled with tears, like Eliza's—were seeing the love of my life wearing my mother's wedding dress. I vividly remembered telling my cousin that she could take it since I'd never have any use for it. I was so thankful now that she had asked.

I looked down at the dress shirt I was wearing along with corduroy trousers and a tweed jacket. "Do I look alright?" I asked Hammer.

"You could use a tie," said the vicar.

Hammer removed his by loosening it and pulling it over his head. "Hang on a sec," I heard him say as I turned around, put it under my shirt collar, and tightened it. "Okay, he's ready."

Eliza handed Harper one of the bouquets of flowers that had been wrapped with ribbon, and she came to stand beside me.

I knew I was supposed to look at the vicar when he spoke, but I couldn't take my eyes off the woman I already considered my wife.

He recited words we each repeated, said a prayer, and gave us his blessing as he said, "On behalf of God, our Father, I now pronounce you man and wife."

When he told me to hurry up and kiss her, I took full advantage, kissing her more deeply, with more love, than I ever had before.

"Time to celebrate!" exclaimed Eliza, who rushed into the kitchen and came back out with a tray of glasses filled with champagne.

"Hang on," said Hammer. "We have some paper-work to sign before the bride, groom, and their two witnesses partake in any alcohol."

"Along with the marriage license," said the vicar.

I snaked my arm around Harper's waist and kissed the side of her neck. "I have never seen a vision as breathtaking as you in that dress."

She turned in my arms. "There's something I need to do." When she led me out of the room, I shrugged at Hammer's inquisitive expression.

I followed her into the bedroom and closed the door behind me.

Harper took a deep breath and let it out slowly. "I don't know if you're comfortable with this sort of thing, but it would mean a lot to me if we could pray together."

"Of course. Nothing would mean more to me."

She held my hands, and we faced each other. When Harper didn't close her eyes, neither did I.

"Heavenly Father, thank you for bringing this man into my life. Thank you for making my every dream come true. For giving me a loving husband, a place to spread the word of Your Grace, and a family. Protect my husband, my Saint, my Niven. Keep him safe in your loving arms and deliver him back here to me as soon as you possibly can. Amen."

"Amen." I was speechless, not just from her words but also at the wonder of the miracle that stood before me. Telling her I loved her didn't seem like enough, but I said the words anyway. "I love you, Harper."

"I love you, Saint."

Harper and I returned to the living room and signed the papers Hammer had spread out on the table. He indicated where we needed to initial as he read the contents aloud. When we finished, Hammer asked Eliza and the vicar to join us so he and the former could sign the marriage certificate as our witnesses.

"We'll take the vicar next door," said Eliza, kissing my cheek. "Dinner will be delivered at five, so when someone knocks, put on your knickers and answer the door."

I laughed. "You are a minx, but I love you, cousin."

"I love you too, Niven."

"Where are you off to, then?"

"I'm driving Hammer back to London tonight, but I'll return as soon as I hear from you." I watched as she hugged and kissed Harper. I thanked Hammer again for coming all this way, but didn't encourage him to stay, at least at the cottage. I was too anxious to get our wedding night underway.

Harper and I spent two blissful days and nights in our cottage before the call came from Decker that the team had been assembled and was waiting for me in London.

The hardest thing I'd ever done was to bid my love farewell, get in the car, and drive away as she and my cousin stood in the doorway, waving.

33

Saint

I placed a call asking Rip to gather the team, have them collect their gear, and advise them we'd meet at the Wellesley, where I'd give a briefing before we prepared for our departure.

"Hello, Saint," said Angel, approaching me first when I walked in the door of the suite. "I hear congratulations are in order."

I raised a brow and then lowered it when I saw Hammer standing on the other side of the room. He raised a glass and walked in my direction. "What's he still doing here?" I asked.

"He's on the team."

"What's this? You aren't really going to Sunderban?"

"Sure as hell am. I promised Harper I'd make sure you didn't do anything stupid."

"No offense, mate, but—"

"Welcome to the Invincibles, Saint." Rip walked up and clapped Hammer's shoulder. "Where you never underestimate your teammates."

Hammer pulled out the cigar he often carried with him but I'd never seen him light. "Colonel, retired. Former commander. Marine Raider Regiment and Marine Corps Force Recon."

"I'd no idea."

"Need-to-know, man. Why do you think we're considered the best? Because we don't brag about it."

The two separate and distinct units were both considered the most elite of all US military units.

"A moment, Saint," said Rip, who led me into another of the suite's rooms. "There's been a development."

"Go on."

"When we arrive in Kolkata, we'll be joined by members of MARCOS."

"By whose authority?"

"Yours. But at the request of Decker Ashford and Z Alexander."

"I see."

"Should I get everyone ready to leave?"

"Yes. Say, Rip? I just wanted you to know I'm honored to be working with you again."

"Likewise, Saint."

While the group prepared for our departure, I needed a few minutes to process Rip's news.

MARCOS, short for India's Marine Commandos, were considered to be the deadliest of all special forces. While the Marine Raiders were considered the best in the US, MARCOS claimed that title on a worldwide level. They trained with US Navy SEALs, the British SAS, and finally in guerrilla warfare in Vairangte, India. They operated under extreme secrecy and had carried out some of recent history's most important and deadly ops.

"I've been awaiting your call," said Z when I rang.

"What's this about MARCOS?"

"They insisted."

"Why?"

"You'll be on their soil, Saint. Oh, and Deck's waiting to hear from you too. When he does, he'll establish a secure video connection so you can review your plan with them before your arrival in Kolkata."

"Roger that."

"Godspeed, Saint."

Before getting in touch with Decker, I went over the plan I'd crafted with the team as it now stood—including two MARCOS soldiers, Sanjay and Ramesh.

After Rip, Hammer, and Angel, I looked into the eyes of Ink, Jagger, Rock, and Crash as I reiterated my instructions to extract Adam Benjamin and Jinyan Tai Man and return them to the UK. Both were to be kept alive by any and every means possible.

We'd travel by plane from London to Netaji Subhas Chandra Bose Airport in Kolkata. From there, a transport, led by MARCOS as was confirmed by Sanjay, would take us to Sagar Island, where we'd go by waterway into the tiger reserve.

The mission wasn't unlike the one in China, where we'd flown from Los Angeles to Taiwan, took seaplanes over the China Sea to the Zhoushan Archipelago, and then boats to Gongqing Forest Park, where the American spy was being held in one of China's black jails.

The biggest difference between the two ops was that we hadn't had to navigate a reserve that was home to hundreds of man-eating Bengal tigers in order to retrieve our targets.

Not that tigers were the only dangerous species we'd encounter. The Sundarbans were also home to king cobras, common cobras, banded kraits, and vipers. They were the venomous ones. The python, chequered keelback, dhaman, and green whip snake weren't poisonous but just as deadly. Not to mention crocodiles and six species of sharks.

By comparison, the perils faced by heroes in adventure movies seemed like child's play. Benjamin and Jinyan couldn't have chosen a more civilized place to hide out, could they? Say Mongolia?

While our tactical gear might protect us from a snake's venomous bite, it certainly wouldn't from strangulation or a crocodile or tiger attack.

Flight time on the first leg of our journey was ten hours. Ground travel from Kolkata to Sagar Island would take another four, and then from the island into the waters of the reserve would take at least another three.

Based on Decker's coordinates of Jinyan's location, we'd have slightly under twenty minutes of traversing through the dense, narrow creeks of the nearly impenetrable mangrove forests.

I studied the aerial surveillance footage Decker had provided of the encampment. While our journey there would be quite harried, the destination looked more like a resort.

There appeared to be four thatch-roofed huts, no more than two hundred square feet each. Several all-terrain vehicles were parked in and around the structures. In all of the images, only two people were ever visible. Zooming in, I immediately recognized Adam Benjamin. His hand was on the shoulder of another man, who looked the right age to be his son, Tai Man.

The only thing that gave me pause was the full-grown white Bengal tiger that looked to be roaming freely around them.

As I'd anticipated, the two men from MARCOS had their own idea of how the mission should be carried out. Since I was the only person, other than Decker, currently in possession of the true coordinates of the encampment, I was prepared to allow them to escort us to the vicinity, but that was it. This was my mission, not theirs. I bloody well didn't care whose soil we were on.

While the world believed MARCOS were the best, looking at my assembled crew, I knew we were better. They might be deadlier, but we knew how to extract and keep the targets alive.

Before we left Kolkata, I instructed Crash and Angel to remain on standby while the rest of us split up. Rip, Rock, and Jagger comprised team one. Hammer, Ink, and I, team two. Each group was responsible for securing one target. Team one: Tai Man. Team two: his father. In hindsight, I should've assigned myself to Tai Man since I was ready to kill Adam Benjamin with my bare hands.

His motive for going into Hong Kong before he and I had the chance to meet was obvious. His plan all along had been to get my attention so that when he deployed, I would be prepared to follow. Benjamin's desired outcome was equally obvious. He wanted his son extracted out of India and taken to the UK, where he'd be given asylum. Somehow, I doubted the peaceful father-son, happily-ever-after existence he was hoping for was rooted in any semblance of reality.

My prediction was Jinyan would allow us close enough to get Benjamin, if only so the man was out of his hair. Otherwise, he would die rather than agree to come with us.

Less than an hour from the reserve, I couldn't stop the vision of Harper from invading my thoughts. She was always there, in the back of my mind, but I knew the only way to stay alive was to stay focused on the mission. *Only* the mission.

"You okay?" asked Hammer.

I nodded.

"Eye on the prize, man."

His comment reminded me of the words Rile had said to me the day of his wedding. "Keep your eye on the tiger's."

While most missions were carried out under the cover of night, this one would be safer midday when predators were resting. I tested my NVGs, which I wouldn't need until later, if at all, earpiece and mic, as well as my GPS. I watched as the others did the same.

Moments later, we jumped off either side of the boat, split into two teams, and crept into the jungle, followed by one MARCOS soldier each as our cover.

Once we got close, we'd take our positions and wait for team one to give us a read on how many threats we were dealing with on their side—human and otherwise. "Be on the lookout for a lone tiger," I warned. "Seemingly domesticated."

The closer we got to the so-called encampment, the more my instincts told me something was off. As

I inched closer, I could see Adam and another man, presumably his son, seated in the center of the clearing. Every so often, they'd look around as if they were expecting someone to join them.

"No one in any of the structures on this side," reported Rip after scanning both of them with the handheld Doppler radar device that worked like a finely tuned motion detector, using radio waves to zero in on movements as slight as human breathing.

"No one over here either," reported Jagger. "Just the two visible targets."

"What in the bloody hell is happening?" I muttered into my mic at the same moment I heard a roar coming from behind me. I spun around and watched in horror as a white Bengal came barreling toward me.

Rile's words echoed in my head as I stared the tiger in the eye, pulled my sidearm, and popped off five rounds that hit their mark but did nothing to stop him.

34

Harper

"I'll leave you and the vicar to chat," said Eliza when we returned to the cottage after visiting with the head of the University of Sussex Theology department.

"I would say that went quite well," said Reverend Primrose—Oliver, as he insisted I call him.

"All that's left is to get my student visa, and I'll be ready to start classes right after Epiphany."

He studied me. "Your mind is elsewhere, my child."

I stood and looked out the window at the garden. I closed my eyes and willed the image of Saint, our baby, and me together there, but it wouldn't come.

It had been three days since he left, and while I hadn't expected to receive word, it seemed with every hour that passed, it became harder for me to conjure the image I hoped would ease my worry.

"Harper, come here."

I walked over to where the reverend sat in his wheel-chair. "What can I bring you?"

"Sit and pray with me, Harper. Pray hard."

35

Saint

Just as the tiger was about to pounce, a shot rang out over my head, and I watched the beast fall to the ground less than two feet in front of me.

I spun around and came face-to-face with the man who'd just saved my life. "Thank you," I said, bending at the waist and putting my hands on my knees to catch my breath.

"Lower your weapon," I heard Hammer say to the man whose gun was still trained on me.

"Stand down," I said to him and Rip. "This man saved my life."

When I stood, I saw Ink, Jagger, and Rock approaching from the other side of the open area, along with Adam Benjamin.

"I know your father," I said to the man, who lowered the gun I recognized as a .458 Rigby.

Adam stopped walking a few yards from us. "This is the man I told you about, my son."

Tai Man nodded and motioned with his hand toward one of the huts. "Come with me."

"Stand down," I repeated when I saw Hammer and Rip both take a step in our direction.

"I don't have much to offer," he said once we were inside. He raised a bottle that looked like whiskey.

"Please."

He poured a glass and handed it to me before filling his own. "You were foolish to come into the reserve."

I studied him. "I came for your father."

He shook his head. "He is the bigger fool."

"I came for you as well."

"I should've let the tiger kill you."

"Why didn't you? I sense the beast meant something to you."

"My father lured you here. The tiger—merely a predator."

I doubted that but nodded. "He grew impatient with me. I promised to help him find you." I looked into the eyes of Tai Man, who I'd always imagined to be younger than me, even when I knew his actual age was a few years older. He sounded and looked more like his father than I imagined he would, his features more

European than Asian, his accent more like someone raised in the UK. His hair was gray like Adam's, his skin weathered, his eyes weary. I watched as he stood and poured us each another drink.

"He wants you to return to England with him."

Tai Man sat down and motioned for me to do the same.

"There is nothing in England for me."

"There's your father."

He sighed. "I suppose he is all that's left."

"I was sorry to hear of your mother's passing."

"She is in a better place."

"I'm curious. What brought you to Sundarbans?"

He laughed. "I figured no one could get to me here, or at least they'd be discouraged from trying."

"Your father is a very determined man."

He nodded. "Saint, right?"

"Yes. Niven St. Thomas, but most call me Saint."

"He considers you his other son."

I ran my hand through my hair and stood. "May I?" I asked, pointing to the bottle. He nodded and held up his glass. I poured us both another.

"What happens next?" he asked.

"We leave."

"Who leaves?"

"That's dependent upon whether you or your father want to travel with us."

He motioned up and down at my gear with his hand that held his glass. "You came ready to take us either way."

I shrugged and downed my whiskey. "That was before you saved my life."

His eyes scrunched. "What would happen if I said I wasn't going anywhere?"

"With me? Nothing. With your father? I can't answer that."

He nodded.

"I'm curious about something."

"What is that?"

"How in bloody hell did he get here?"

Tai Man leaned forward and rested his elbows on his knees. For the first time since we came inside, he smiled. "Helicopter."

36

Harper

When it rang, I grabbed the phone I kept by my side every second. "Saint?"

"Hello, my darling."

"Where are you?"

"We've just landed at Heathrow. I'll be on my way to you as soon as I'm off this damned plane."

"It's one in the morning. Are you sure you don't want to rest first?"

"It is, isn't it? I've woken you, haven't I?"

"Saint?"

"Yes, my darling?"

"Are you okay?"

"Better now that I've heard your voice."

"Me too."

"I'll be there as soon as I can."

"Be safe."

"Always."

When the call ended, I closed my eyes, and the image of my beloved husband, our baby, and me out in our garden was the dream I fell asleep to.

The dream soon changed. Instead of being in the garden, Saint and I were in bed together. I could feel him naked against my back, his arms wrapped around my waist. He moved my hair, and I shuddered when he kissed my neck. I knew he'd soon tell me to be still, but for now, my body writhed against his.

"Harper, my love," he whispered, and my eyes sprung open.

"You're here!" I exclaimed, twisting in his arms so I could look into his eyes and feel his lips on mine. I cupped his cheek with my palm. "I'm so glad you're home, so glad you're safe. I was so worried."

"All in one piece," he said with a grin, pulling me against his hardness.

"I know I'm not supposed to ask."

"But?"

"Were you able to find Dr. Benjamin and his son?"

"I was."

"Are they safe too?"

"Very much so."

I rested my head on his chest. "I'm happy it went so well, but happier that nothing happened to you and that you're home safe and sound."

He kissed the top of my head but didn't say anything.

"Saint? Nothing happened to you, right?"

"Well, there was the bit with the tiger. However, I followed Rile's advice and stared him in the eye."

I looked up at his grin and swatted his chest. "Stop teasing and make love to me."

"It would be my divine pleasure, my darling Harper."

Epilogue

Saint

Today Harper and I would celebrate our marriage with family and friends.

Given so many of the Invincibles would be traveling from the States, Decker had arranged for a private plane to leave from DC. Thus, Harper's mother, father, stepmother, and best friend could catch the flight if they wished to. All were on board, a fact that made my wife happy and unhappy at the same time. It was her nature to forgive her father regardless of his lack of apology. That didn't mean she'd forgotten his treatment of her. When we discussed whether to invite him or not, her worry was she'd one day regret not having her father at our celebration.

"I hope someone made sure the douche didn't get on the plane."

I laughed out loud at Harper's use of the disparaging "nickname."

"I'm quite sure he did not."

"You never know with my father, although Mouse would've murdered both of them if he had."

"I cannot wait to meet her."

"Thank you for inviting her and my mother to stay here."

"It is my pleasure, my darling."

She beamed at me. "And for not inviting my father and his wife."

I'd considered booking a room for them several towns over, or even in London, so their stay in Alfriston would be brief, but in the end, let them handle their own travel arrangements besides the flight here.

The other thing I'd considered was informing Harper's dad that while my employer had arranged for their air travel to London, they would be on their own getting back.

When I suggested it to Harper, she giggled but made it clear I shouldn't give in to dastardly thoughts.

"'It is mine to avenge; I will repay,' says the Lord," she said, reminding me again of her uncanny way of soothing my soul. Even if it meant guarding it.

She'd decided not to pursue her degree at university until after our baby was born next summer. She did, however, take on her role as curate with vigor.

Reverend Primrose gave her three of the five churches to minister to during Advent, and took the two closest to Alfriston himself. Thus, I was able to experience the magic of the Christmas celebration three times over. I'd do it one hundred times again just to see the joy it brought my wife.

Not only did it bring Harper joy, but it also kept her busy enough that she didn't have as much time to fret over our guests' arrival. Eliza had taken on the planning of the reception celebration that was to be held tonight, New Year's Eve.

It was early for guests to be arriving or for the caterers to start setting up, so I had no idea who might be knocking on our door. I was delighted when I opened it to find Adam Benjamin and his son standing on our threshold. "Come in, come in. What a pleasant surprise."

"We're early," said Tai Man. "But we don't plan to stay."

"Oh. You're coming back later, though, yes?"

"We wouldn't miss it," said Adam.

"So, um, can I get you anything?" I motioned for them to step into the living room at the same time Harper came out of the bedroom.

"Adam, Tai Man, it is such a pleasure to see you!" She stepped forward and cheek-kissed each man, then met my gaze. I gave a discreet shrug.

"I would prefer to offer my wedding gifts to you in private," said the man who'd saved my life.

"By all means. Thank you."

Tai Man stepped forward and presented a box to Harper.

"May I open it now?" she asked.

He held up one finger and turned to me. He gave me a box too, much smaller than hers. "Go ahead," he said to both of us.

I would normally have waited until my wife had opened her gift, but Tai Man's insistence that he give us the boxes at the same time dictated otherwise.

I raised the lid and smiled. I looked down at the corded leather that held a single tiger claw. "Many thanks." My voice was too clogged with emotion to say anything else.

I glanced at Harper's expression and then looked at what was beneath the lid of her box. The Victorian-looking necklace was made from eight claws similar to the one Tai Man had given me. They were mounted in gold and strung on a delicate gold chain.

"In my mother's culture, a tiger claw is the emblem of dignity, ferocity, sternness, and courage. We believe it is a symbol of protection."

Harper, wide-eyed and with a look of awe, turned from me to Tai Man. "I don't know how to thank you. This means so much."

Little did she know the truth of her statement. If it weren't for the man standing before me, I wouldn't be alive. I also wouldn't have ventured into the tiger reserve in the first place, but that was a sentiment meant for the next time the two of us met to share a glass of whiskey—an occurrence made more frequent by the asylum and subsequent protection the UK had granted him.

Tai Man leaned in closer to Harper, and I heard him whisper. "The claw of a white tiger, in particular, is said to ward off quarrels."

Her eyes briefly met mine, and she smiled before her cheeks pinked and she cast her gaze downward. Little did my friend know that Harper already had the means to diffuse any disagreement by that look alone, particularly when she showed me her dimples.

Keep reading for a sneak peek at the
next book in the Invincibles series:
Hammered

1

Hammer

When I saw Money McTiernan's name show up on my cell shortly after my flight landed in Dallas, I let it go to voicemail. What could he possibly need to talk to me about now, anyway? It hadn't been that long since we went our separate ways after traveling to DC from London following Saint and Harper's wedding celebration. Not to mention, it was eight in the morning and I hadn't gotten any sleep on either plane ride.

My phone vibrated again, this time with a text message.

Urgent I speak with you asap, it read.

"Fuck," I muttered under my breath, wishing I could wait until I'd gotten some rest to respond. However, that was out of the question. As the Invincibles' attorney of record, I had no choice but to answer when one of them called with something urgent. While Money didn't work for the organization directly, he was our primary contact at the CIA, which meant he counted.

"What can I do for you, Money?" I asked when he picked up.

"My sister needs some legal help."

She better be in lockup for him to send me a message saying it was urgent he speak with me. "What's going on?"

"She's buying a bar and the owner tried to renegotiate the sale last night."

"And?"

"She shot him."

About the Author

USA Today and Amazon Top 15 Bestselling Author Heather Slade writes shamelessly sexy, edge-of-your seat romantic suspense.

She gave herself the gift of writing a book for her own birthday one year. Forty-plus books later (and counting), she's having the time of her life.

The women Slade writes are self-confident, strong, with wills of their own, and hearts as big as the Colorado sky. The men are sublimely sexy, seductive alphas who rise to the challenge of capturing the sweet soul of a woman whose heart they'll hold in the palm of their hand forever. Add in a couple of neck-snapping twists and turns, a page-turning mystery, and a swoon-worthy HEA, and you'll be holding one of her books in your hands.

She loves to hear from my readers. You can contact her at heather@heatherslade.com

To keep up with her latest news and releases, please visit her website at www.heatherslade.com to sign up for her newsletter.

MORE FROM AUTHOR HEATHER SLADE

BUTLER RANCH
Kade's Worth
Brodie's Promise
Maddox's Truce
Naughton's Secret
Mercer's Vow
Kade's Return
Butler Ranch Christmas

WICKED WINEMAKERS
FIRST LABEL
Brix's Bid
Ridge's Release
Press' Passion
Zin's Sins
Tryst's Temptation

WICKED WINEMAKERS
SECOND LABEL
Beau's Beloved
Coming Soon:
Cru's Crush
Bones' Bliss
Snapper's Seduction
Kick's Kiss

ROARING FORK RANCH
Coming Soon:
Roaring Fork Wrangler
Roaring Fork Roughstock
Roaring Fork Rockstar
Roaring Fork Rooker
Roaring Fork Bridger

THE ROYAL AGENTS
OF MI6
Make Me Shiver
Drive Me Wilder
Feel My Pinch
Chase My Shadow
Find My Angel

K19 SECURITY
SOLUTIONS TEAM ONE
Razor's Edge
Gunner's Redemption
Mistletoe's Magic
Mantis' Desire
Dutch's Salvation

K19 SECURITY
SOLUTIONS TEAM TWO
Striker's Choice
Monk's Fire
Halo's Oath
Tackle's Honor
Onyx's Awakening

K19 SHADOW OPERATIONS
TEAM ONE
Code Name: Ranger
Code Name: Diesel
Code Name: Wasp
Code Name: Cowboy
Code Name: Mayhem

K19 ALLIED INTELLIGENCE
TEAM ONE
Code Name: Ares
Code Name: Cayman
Code Name: Poseidon
Code Name: Zeppelin
Code Name: Magnet

K19 ALLIED INTELLIGENCE
TEAM TWO
Coming Soon:
Code Name: Puck
Code Name: Michelangelo
Code Name: Typhon
Code Name: Hornet
Code Name: Reaper

PROTECTORS
UNDERCOVER
Undercover Agent
Undercover Emissary
Coming Soon:
Undercover Savior
Undercover Infidel
Undercover Assassin

THE INVINCIBLES
TEAM ONE
Decked
Edged
Grinded
Riled
Smoked

THE INVINCIBLES
TEAM TWO
Bucked
Irished
Sainted
Hammered
Ripped

THE UNSTOPPABLES
TEAM ONE
Furied
Merried

COWBOYS OF
CRESTED BUTTE
A Cowboy Falls
A Cowboy's Dance
A Cowboy's Kiss
A Cowboy Stays
A Cowboy Wins